wicked winemakers

CENTRAL COAST

FIRST LABEL

—BOOK FIVE—

TRYST'S *Temptation*

USA TODAY BESTSELLING AUTHOR

HEATHER SLADE

Table of Contents

Prologue

Jaicon
October

Some called them tears. Others, legs. I observed each drip and its thickness as I held the goblet at an angle, letting the wine flow up one side of the glass, then leveled it, watching as the liquid trailed down. I swirled once more, closed my eyes, then stuck my nose in the glass' bowl and breathed in deeply. Aromas of sage and thyme mingled with the core scent of red fruit, rich with wild strawberry, raspberry, and freshly picked plum, making my mouth water.

I didn't take a drink. I couldn't. I was on the clock.

Instead, I set the glass on the table in front of me. Over its rim, my eyes met Tryst's. I watched as they drifted closed with the first sip. The look on his face was the same I'd seen the night before. Then, he'd raised his head from between my legs.

"This is the wine I crave," he'd said, running his tongue through my folds.

I trembled at the vividness of the image, squeezing my thighs together and wishing I could suggest we leave, return to the cottage by the sea he'd arranged for us to stay in, and make love throughout the night, serenaded by the sound of the waves crashing on the beach below us.

Instead, I had to remain here, staking out a wine-industry charity fundraiser after receiving intel suggesting a key player in a human trafficking ring I'd been investigating for several months was to be in attendance.

While the man's identity was unknown, as with every mission, I scanned the room, relying on instinct—my gut—to recognize someone who posed a threat. It was what I was trained to do, the same way the other operatives positioned around the room were.

I heard the woman who chaired the event, Tryst's niece, announce the start of the Wicked Winemaker bachelor auction.

My eyes met Tryst's again from across the table, and he smiled. I loved his smile. It made me feel warm, safe, treasured. Apparently, Alexis, or Alex as everyone called her, had been after Tryst to participate in the auction the last couple of years. He and I joked that if he did, I'd be forced to take down any woman who bid on him.

"Ladies, I'm thrilled to open the bidding for a date with a man who is a fan favorite year after year: Zin Oliver!" said Alex.

Several paddles raised, but she didn't react. Instead, I heard her say, "Where is she?" to her assistant. Realizing she'd spoken into a hot mic, she gave a quick explanation and flipped it off. Zin walked over to her rather than remain near the catwalk. Seconds later, he jumped from the stage.

"The office!" I heard Zin say through my earpiece.

Simultaneously, I received an alert through the comms from Blackjack, one of the operatives on my team. "Suspect reported in back office. Possible hostage situation."

"Who is the hostage?"

"Jada Yáñez."

"Support needed in rear hallway of the building," I said through the mic of my headset, racing off in that direction.

The woman he mentioned had been abducted and tortured ten months ago by another man affiliated with the trafficking ring. That she was potentially in danger again sent the already surging adrenaline flooding into my bloodstream.

I touched the handle of the door with the tip of my finger. It was locked.

"Jada? The bidding has started. Are you coming out?" I said.

"Sorry. Be right there," she responded.

I drew my gun. "You cover Jada," I whispered to Zin when Tank, my backup, joined us. "Count of three," I added, motioning for him to bust through the door. When it broke from the hinges, Jada screamed.

"*Freeze!*" I shouted, my gun leveled directly at the man standing near the rear of the room. "Hands in the air!" What did the bloody bastard do instead of following my directives? First, the cowardly *sonuvabitch* moved behind Jada, using her as a shield. Then, just as Zin grabbed her and whisked her out of the room, the man reached for his gun. I fired first.

When he hit the ground, I rushed forward.

"Where's the weapon?" Tank knelt to secure it while I checked for a pulse.

"He reached to his right," I said, picturing it in my mind as though I were still in the moment. "He's alive."

I breathed a sigh of relief. The presence of a pulse meant that when he regained consciousness, we might be able to turn him, get him to lead us to whomever he worked for in return for a lesser charge against him.

"There's no gun. No weapon of any kind," I heard Tank say as I called for an ambulance.

"Sorry, what did you say?"

"He was unarmed, Jaicon."

1

Tryst
One year ago

"Tryst, this is Jaicon Heart, code name Esencia," said Kade Butler, a man I'd known most of my life.

A cool autumn breeze swept across the meadow where we stood, but when my hand met hers in greeting, warmth flowed from the top of my head to my toes. Staring into the depths of her violet-blue eyes—the color of the cornflowers that used to grow in the gardens of my home in California—something stirred inside me I never thought would again.

"Most people call me Jacy," she said.

"I am Tryst Avila. Welcome to Mexico and to *El Lugar de Curación.*"

"It's so beautiful here." Jacy looked down at her hand still between both of mine. "It's the Healing Place, yes?"

As much as I wanted to feel her touch a few moments longer, I let go. "Do you speak Spanish?"

"Jaicon speaks several languages," bragged Merrigan, Kade's wife and the managing partner of the private security and intelligence firm they owned.

Even as she and I cheek-kissed, I didn't take my eyes off the woman whose aura captivated me—the woman who had to be half my age. I would've said younger, but that she worked for my two friends meant she had to be older than I might've initially guessed.

"Jacy will be assisting with the reunification process when the trafficking victims arrive later today. I can't thank you enough, Tryst, for allowing us to use your ranch to bring these families back together."

"Ditto," said Kade, putting his arm around his wife. "What these people went through is horrifying and heartbreaking."

The men, women, and children Kade spoke of had been abducted by human traffickers and loaded into shipping containers bound for the UK.

Kade and Merrigan's firm, K19 Security Solutions, was responsible for their rescue once the ship the containers were on landed in the Port of Felixstowe, outside of London.

"It is a small thing compared to what you and your team have done," I said, glancing at my two friends, then at Jaicon. "May I show you to your *casita*?" I asked.

She looked over at her employers.

"Go ahead," said Kade. "We'll find our own way," he added, nudging me with his elbow.

I motioned to a golf cart a short distance from where we stood. My eyes drifted downward from her long wavy blonde hair that, even swept up in a ponytail, touched the small of her back, to the sway of her hips as she walked in front of me. She was dressed simply, in a pair of bottom-hugging jeans, a loose-fitting white T-shirt, and cowboy boots, yet on her, it was…*sexy*.

I ran my hand through my beard, trying to recall the last time I'd had a similar thought about a woman. Not since before my beloved wife, Rosa, was diagnosed with cancer fourteen years ago. She'd been gone ten. Had it truly been that long since I felt desire?

Thinking about my wife should've quelled my reaction to Jaicon, but once I sat beside her on the bench seat of the golf cart, I found myself wanting to lean closer and brush the bare skin on her arm with mine. Instead, I gripped the steering wheel with both hands.

"That is the main house, where I live," I said, pointing to it. "Should you need anything, do not hesitate to knock on my door."

"That's very kind of you." Her smile took my breath away.

"It is my pleasure." I cleared my throat, hating the suggestive tone in my voice.

When I parked the cart in front of the guest *casita*, I wondered if I'd made a wise decision by lodging her in such close proximity. Actually, I knew I hadn't. "How old are you?" I blurted.

Her laughter stunned me back to my senses.

"Forgive me," I murmured.

"Don't apologize. I'm often asked."

I cocked my head. "You are?"

"I'm older than I look."

"I suppose it would be rude of me to ask how much older."

She laughed again. "I'm thirty-two. Thirty-three in December." She cocked her head like I had. "How old are you?"

"I fear it's the opposite for me. I look older than my age."

Her eyes stayed riveted to mine.

"I'll be fifty in January."

I waited for a reaction, but Jaicon just shrugged and got out of the golf cart.

"Let me get that." When I went to grab the handle of her bag, my hand covered hers, sending a jolt of lust surging through my body. I felt as though I should apologize again, but doing so would draw attention to something she may not have noticed.

"It isn't heavy, Tryst. I can manage."

I left my hand where it was. "You're not just saying that because you think I'm an old man, are you?"

"You are *not* an old man." Her words were as emphatic as the look in her eyes.

She pulled her hand out from under mine and stuffed it in the front pocket of her jeans. "I should, um, ring Fatale—I mean, Merrigan—and see when the plane is scheduled to arrive." She lowered her gaze.

My left hand remained on the handle of her bag. I itched to bring my right to her chin and raise her face so I could see her eyes once more. "I've made you uncomfortable."

"No," she said, looking up at me. "Well, maybe."

I felt like such a fool. Worse, a lecherous *old* man. I picked the bag up, carried it to the *casita*, and opened the door. I set it inside, then returned to her. "You'll find the key hanging just inside the entryway. I'll have one of the caretakers stock the refrigerator and pantry whenever it would be the least intrusive. There is a riding center, a meditation room, and a chapel on the property. You are welcome to make use of any of them." I walked beyond the golf cart but motioned to it. "I will leave this here in case you need to use it."

Her mouth opened just slightly, then closed.

"Good afternoon, Jaicon. It was a pleasure to meet you."

"Wait," she said when I was almost at my front door.

I looked over my shoulder. "Yes?"

"I've offended you. It wasn't my intention."

"You have not. I have several nieces and nephews your age. You remind me of them. I forget that not every family is as…affectionate as ours. Again, forgive me." I opened the door, went inside, and rested against its solid wood after I closed it behind me. Shutting my eyes, I raked my hand through my hair.

What had I been thinking? First, I could barely keep my hands off the woman, then I said she reminded me of my nieces. Or niece. I only had one. Not that Jaicon knew that, or ever would. I'd gone from a lecherous old man to a more lecherous old *uncle*.

I opened my eyes and stared up at the ceiling. The words were on the tip of my tongue to ask for Rosa's forgiveness. Somehow, that made my behavior seem worse.

I stalked to the rear door of the house and walked to the meditation center. It was a far enough distance for me to usually take one of the golf carts. Now, though, I needed to walk off the negative energy swirling inside me before I entered the sacred place.

I bowed as I walked through the door, then lit the candles on the Vastu altar before placing a mat on the floor. Rather than begin, as I often did, with *Sukhasana*, I lay flat on my back and focused on merging my thoughts and my present state of agitation.

I took several deep breaths, reminding myself to appreciate my body, my life, and my circumstances— exactly as they were.

I lay one hand on my chest, heart center, then crossed it with the other, letting go of my expectations with every breath I exhaled. Each time I inhaled, I brought in gratitude.

I let go of the passage of time, waiting instead for the calm of stillness to wash over me. Then, I'd be ready to begin. It didn't matter if it took minutes or hours.

When my disquiet evolved into peace, I slowly stood and stretched my neck and shoulders. I turned my head just as the door to the center opened. Jaicon peeked inside, then closed it without coming in.

When I stepped outside just as she was about to get in the golf cart, she sputtered, "I didn't think anyone was here. I'm so sorry to interrupt."

"Wait. Please, don't leave."

Her head was bowed, but she raised it. "I'm sorry," she repeated. "I don't know what happened earlier. If I said or did something—"

The peace I felt stayed with me as I approached her. "The fault is mine," I murmured when I was close enough for her to hear me. Her eyes met mine, and I smiled. "Perhaps we should begin again."

She nodded. "I'd like that."

"Welcome to my ranch, Jaicon."

"Thank you for having me, Tryst."

"Will you join me in the meditation center?"

Her eyes scrunched. "Yes."

I chuckled. "Are you certain?"

She looked out over the landscape, then returned her gaze to mine. "Do I really remind you of your nieces?"

I shook my head. "I have but one, and not even a little."

She smiled. "Then, I'd love to."

2

Jaicon

Trystan Avila had inched his way under my skin within the first moments of meeting him. I'd never once, in my entire life, had such a reaction. Even when I first met my husband—the person I'd once believed would be the only man I ever loved.

Given my profession, my instincts were finely honed. I could pick up on suspect behavior in seconds. However, this was entirely different, leaving me unsure what to make of it.

I *wanted* Tryst Avila. How long had it been since I'd felt that way? *Three years.*

When he lay flat on a yoga mat after placing a second on the floor for me, my first thought was to rest my body on top of his. After stripping us both of our clothes, of course.

When he'd mentioned the meditation center, earlier, I immediately knew it was where I wanted to go. *Needed* to go in order to recenter myself. Doing so now was impossible. Not with him right beside me.

I closed my eyes, attempting to calm myself. As hard as I tried to focus on my breathing, all I could hear was his. He assaulted the rest of my senses as well.

His scent was sensual, refined, and masculine. Like orris root combined with sage, jasmine, and warm sandalwood. Perhaps something else nutty, like roasted almonds.

When his hand had rested on mine, it felt soft yet calloused like that of a man who wasn't afraid of hard work. His touch left me breathless.

Staring into his eyes, I saw so many things. Wisdom, playfulness, curiosity, and above all else—desire. His comment about looking older than his age was ridiculous. Even fully dressed, the hard outline of his toned muscles was evident. Truth be told, the entirety of the man caused my heart to pound, as if our souls had collided the very instant we met.

I longed to touch his hand that rested so close to mine it would've taken only the slightest movement to make it happen.

"Jaicon?"

His voice startled me, and I gulped. "Yes?"

"I can feel your thoughts."

"Sorry," I whispered, wishing I hadn't and hoping he hadn't heard. I glanced over at his grin, knowing he had.

"Don't be. I like them."

If I were the smart woman I believed myself to be, I'd get up and walk out, perhaps go as far as to leave the ranch. Those honed instincts of mine were screaming that Tryst Avila spelled all kinds of trouble for me. Particularly given what I already knew of the man.

Like me, he'd lost his spouse. Mine was more recent; Tryst's wife had died a decade ago. They'd met when they were both in their early twenties and married shortly after. "Love at first sight," the dossier quoted him saying.

Tragically, she was diagnosed with pancreatic cancer in her late thirties. The aggressive form of the disease was often incurable, which had been the case with Tryst's wife.

There was no mention of a relationship since she passed. He lived a relatively solitary life in Mexico but frequently traveled to the Central Coast of California. He was a past member of and current advisor to a "good guy" vigilante society known as Los Caballeros. The group had existed in "secret" for several generations, first in Spain, then in the States.

Nothing in what I'd read gave any indication that he was a womanizer. It seemed more to the contrary. Had I misconstrued an innocent conversation to be something more? Was my attraction one-sided?

"These thoughts, I do not like as much."

"Stop it," I said, laughing.

"Your aura is powerful, Jaicon."

I raised a brow. "As is yours, Tryst."

He sat up. "I fear meditation is out of the question for both of us."

"I should return to the *casita*, anyway."

"I will go with you."

I wanted to tell him it would defeat the purpose of my wanting to put space between us. However, my desire to spend even a few more minutes close to him compelled me to keep my mouth shut.

"What?" I asked, noticing his grin had broadened.

Tryst reached out and touched my chin. "Do not bite your tongue, Jaicon."

The rest of the day was hectic with the arrival of those rescued from the ten shipping containers in Port Felixstowe. A total of one hundred and eighty-three people had been transported to the ranch via private planes. Our job was to find out where each person was from and reunite them with their families. Given many were refugees who'd traveled to Mexico from other parts of the world, that process would not be easy.

A few spoke English, but the majority were either Spanish- or French-speaking. Some, who were from Haiti, spoke Haitian Creole.

Many of the operatives helping victims spoke fluent French or Spanish. Creole was more difficult. So I kept busy, assisting as best I could. And, while my stated purpose was to aid in reunification, questioning the victims about their experiences in order to identify suspects was a more accurate description of my mandate. Thus, I walked a fine line in my interaction with the victims.

On one hand, the people I spoke with had been through enough. The last thing any of us wanted to do was make them feel uncomfortable. However, in order to prevent a similar crime from happening to others, finding the perpetrators of the abductions was imperative.

Every so often, my eyes would meet Tryst's, who was working side by side with the physicians K19 had arranged to provide care for those needing it. Even from a distance, I could sense his kindness and how it affected those with whom he spoke.

That he'd agreed to house everyone who arrived here for as long as they needed was admirable in itself. With anyone else, I may have wondered if they knew what they were getting themselves into. Not with Tryst, though. I sensed he would honor his offer regardless of what was eventually required.

It was close to sunset, and I was making notes on a tablet about the last woman I'd spoken with when I felt a hand on my shoulder. Knowing it was Tryst without needing to look, I almost rested my head against it.

"How are you holding up, Jaicon?" he asked.

I looked at those assembled for the dinner Tryst had arranged to be served. Most appeared haggard and emotional. No different than I would've been had I gone through a similar experience. "Better than they are."

He stepped closer, brushing the front of his body against my back. "What they've experienced is unimaginable, and yet, they are so brave."

"For the majority, their arduous journey began long before their abduction."

"You should take a break." Before he removed his hand, his fingers gently kneaded my trapezius. "You have been on your feet for several hours."

I looked over my shoulder. "As have you."

"Then, we should both take a break. Will you join me for dinner?"

I followed him over to the buffet line, waiting until the last of the "guests," as Tryst so kindly referred to them, had been served.

"Where will they stay? Is there room?" I asked, feeling guilty I had a two-bedroom *casita* to myself.

"Between my ranch and those of my neighbors, we can comfortably accommodate everyone here. Merrigan arranged for clothing, shoes, and other incidentals to be delivered prior to their arrival. Each of the guesthouses has been stocked with food and whatever else I could think of they might need."

Tryst asked if we could join one of the tables with two open spots. By the end of our meal, he had every person—man or woman—seated with us hanging on his every word.

When he returned from the buffet line with several helpings of dessert, I teased him, saying, "You are an incorrigible flirt."

"The truth is, I love women. I'll make no apology for it," he responded, winking. "In fact, I love all people."

"Perhaps the word I should've used was admirable."

"You are no different. You love people as much as I do."

I shook my head. "Not true. I have come across many I abhor. For example, the men and women responsible for the pain and suffering of those around us."

"Those who harm others. You make a good point. But is there no chance for redemption?"

"When there is atonement."

He nodded, stroking his beard with his hand. "The Hindus believe a soul's next incarnation depends on the actions throughout a person's previous life."

"Karma."

He studied me. "Are you a believer?"

"In Karma, yes. In reincarnation, I cannot say definitively." I took a bite of tres leches cake, savoring its sweetness and wondering if Tryst was a devout practitioner. If so, what did he believe became of his late wife's soul? "What?" I asked, noticing him staring at my mouth.

"You have a little cream right…here." He reached out and touched my face with his thumb. When he brought it to his lips, I nearly orgasmed. Maybe not *nearly*. However, I was definitely aroused.

"I should, um, probably…" God, what was wrong with me? There were undoubtedly things I needed to do. Why couldn't I think of a single one?

"I'm slowly learning the Esencia sutra," he murmured.

"Slowly?" I muttered. "You haven't known me twenty-four hours."

Tryst's lazy, seductive smile multiplied the desire I felt for him. When he leaned closer, a chill went up my spine. "Perhaps our souls have known each other far longer."

"Incorrigible," I repeated, getting up from the table. "Thank you for an enjoyable meal. I'm sure I'll see you in the morning."

"I will look forward to it."

"You and Tryst seem to be getting on well," said Merrigan when I joined her and Kade—who I knew as Doc—at their table.

"I have rarely encountered a bigger flirt."

"And that would be my cue to leave," said Doc, standing and walking in the direction from where I'd come.

"I don't think he is," said Merrigan, shaking her head.

"Is what?"

"Flirtatious."

I laughed. "You wouldn't say that if you knew him."

"Actually, I know him quite well."

I sobered. "I'm here to do a job."

Merrigan reached across the table and put her hand on mine. "Jaicon, I adore you."

"Uh-oh."

She laughed. "You do know there is more to life than your job, yes? I worry that since—"

I held up my hand. "I do know there's more to life. However, I am here to work. As are you." I sighed. "Besides, Tryst Avila is…not my type."

Merrigan smirked. "How could he be? I mean, he's suave, handsome, with a body that looks sculpted from marble. What else? He's intelligent, enlightened, kind, generous, and owns a ten-thousand-acre ranch."

"Twenty."

She raised a brow.

"It was in the dossier."

"That's right, and with your photographic memory, you'd remember every word."

I closed my eyes, reopening them slowly. "You know how I feel about that."

Merrigan squeezed my fingers. "I do, and I apologize. I shouldn't have made light of it."

The truth was, my memory was far more a curse than a blessing. Some said there was no such thing as a photographic memory, but as a person who lived with the horrible affliction, I disputed the scientists who'd made such a proclamation.

The worst occurrences of my life played repeatedly inside my head—torturing me endlessly. There were good things too, of course, but crowded in with both were endless other things an ordinary person would never recall. Pointless bits of information, like the color and pattern of the tie my high-school boyfriend wore on our first date. I also remembered his shirt, jacket, and trousers, and one bit of hair on the right side of his head, near his temple, that stuck out. It had annoyed me then. More so now, simply because I never wanted to think of it again. Which was the worst part of it. Not being able to shut it off.

While I knew I wasn't the only person plagued by things I didn't want to remember, I was one of the few tormented by every conceivable recollection.

The absolute worst memory of all was of the day I lost my husband. I remembered every moment in vivid, excruciatingly painful detail.

"Here he comes now," Merrigan murmured.

I looked up and saw Tryst walking toward us. I wasn't sure what to make of his expression, except it was anything but playful or flirtatious. If I had to name it, I would've said troubled.

He nodded at Merrigan. "May I steal our Jaicon away for a moment?"

"By all means," she said, waving her hand.

I looked between the two of them, annoyed that neither had asked me whether I wanted to be "stolen."

"I promise not to keep you long," Tryst said, holding his hand out to me.

When I stood without taking the assistance offered, his fingertips brushed the small of my back, then guided me away from the gathering of tables.

"What did you want to speak with me about?" I asked when he kept walking.

"It's something I want you to see."

He led me up a hillside and, when we reached the top, told me to turn around and look to the west.

"Wow." I gasped at the breathtaking view of the setting sun just before it slipped into the sea.

"You have to time it just right to catch the magic."

I kept watching even after all there was to see was an orange glow. "Thank you for bringing me here," I said.

"You looked like you needed some magic."

I smiled, gazing into his eyes. "I did, in fact."

He stepped closer. "May I ask what made you so sad?"

"It wasn't sadness as much as resignation."

He remained silent but fixated.

"I know how this sounds…"

"Tell me anyway."

"I have what's referred to as a photographic memory. Believe me, I've heard all the comments—how lucky I must've been at university, not to have to study for my exams. Things like that. It isn't something I consider lucky."

"I would imagine not."

I cocked my head. "It's rare someone understands without further explanation."

"There are many things I choose not to remember. I cannot imagine how difficult it must be not to have the choice."

"That's *exactly* it." I glanced over my shoulder at the spot where the sun had disappeared. "On the other hand, I'll never forget this."

"The first time I visited, it was this sight that convinced me I had to make this my home."

"I can see why it would." I felt his eyes on me and turned my head. "You're supposed to be looking at this spectacular view," I said, waving my hand.

"I am."

I smiled and shook my head. "I told Merrigan I thought you were a terrible flirt."

"How did she respond?"

"She said you weren't."

"I doubt you'll believe this, but she is right." He took a deep breath and let it out slowly. "With you, I can't help myself."

3

Tryst

I sat on the *terraza* behind my house, winding down from the day. As tired as I should feel, I didn't. My body, my brain, and my soul were filled with too many other emotions. I felt unsettled, anxious, perplexed, and above all else, desirous.

Meeting Jaicon "Esencia" Heart had stirred things inside me I never thought I'd feel again. Now that I had, I couldn't say it made me happy.

Before she and I walked down the hill, her to the guest *casita* and me to my house, she'd said I was a terrible flirt. Earlier, she'd said incorrigible.

Merrigan spoke the truth when she disputed the opinion Jaicon had shared. I *wasn't* the kind of man to come on to women. I'd believed that part of me died with Rosa—the only woman I'd ever loved, ever desired in an all-consuming way.

What a fool I'd made of myself earlier by doing the very thing I'd said I didn't do. I behaved like a smitten teenager with a woman seventeen years my junior. Thankfully, there weren't many witnesses to my idiocy.

This behavior was not indicative of how I saw myself. Who I believed myself to be. Yet, I longed to touch Jaicon, to kiss her, to remove her clothes piece by piece until she stood naked before me. Then I wished to memorize every inch of her body, know it with my eyes, my hands, my lips, and my tongue. I wanted to spend countless hours getting to know everything about her—how she thought, what she liked, her dreams.

Yet, if I chose to act on my attraction, what would happen? *Nothing.* There was more than our age difference to prevent us from having a relationship. While I owned other properties, primarily in California, I was a rancher who lived in Mexico and ran an equine rehabilitation program started by my late wife. Jaicon was a covert operative for a private intelligence firm whose work took her all over the world. Could our day-to-day lives be more disparate?

What did that leave? A physical attraction? I wasn't the kind of man who believed in meaningless sex. I didn't as a young man, and I certainly didn't now. Since there was no possibility of any other kind of relationship between us, the best thing I could do was keep my distance.

I shook my head and chuckled to myself. Here I was, deciding to stay away from a woman who would have no interest in interacting with me anyway.

"Foolish old man," I muttered, staring into the waning fire. Rather than throw another log on, I'd let it die out, go inside, and perhaps read until my brain settled itself. Thus was my life, and it was comfortable.

On instinct, I looked up when I heard a door open and saw Jaicon approach the half wall that surrounded the *terraza* of the guest *casita*. There was enough light from the moon for me to see her rest her hands on the stone and look up at the night sky.

The silhouette of her body made me instantly hard. With the coolness of the air, her nipples would show through the thin shirt she wore. If I stood behind her, I'd capture them between my fingers as I ground my hardness into the crevice between the cheeks of her ass. I'd reach around and cup her pussy, knowing before I did that I'd feel her wetness on my palm. She'd writhe when I kissed the soft skin of her neck, driving us both to an undeniable mad desire.

I adjusted my jeans, but nothing helped the ache in my cock. I'd go inside if I thought I could without her seeing me.

Instead, Jaicon did. Disappointment and relief warred inside me. I was a man who prided himself on his control, but when it came to her, I had none. Maybe keeping my distance while she was here at the ranch wouldn't be enough. Perhaps my leaving for the duration of her stay would be for the best.

Several days later, I'd done neither. I sought Jaicon out at every opportunity. I helped with things she didn't need assistance with. I invented reasons to show her areas on the ranch she may find of interest. All the while, the battle inside me waged on. I fought the urge to touch her every moment I was with her. And yet, I couldn't stay away. I couldn't bear to be more than a few feet from the beguiling woman.

She was exceptionally intelligent, with a sharp intuition that allowed her to quickly assess the mental and emotional state of those she spoke with. As Merrigan had said, she seemed well-versed in several languages and spoke Spanish and French fluently. Above all else, it was her kindness that touched me the most. She freely gave affection and comfort to those who hadn't been able to connect with their families or whose ordeal continued to plague them.

The cost to her, personally, was evident to me, but I doubted others noticed.

"She needs to take a break, Tryst," Merrigan said, walking up to me as I watched Jaicon.

I put my arm around my friend's shoulders. "Getting her to do so will take the metaphoric army."

"Kade and I need to return to California this afternoon." She sighed. "Will you look after her, Tryst?"

"I will." While my gaze rested on Jaicon, I could feel Merrigan watching me.

"I've known her since she completed training at Fort Monckton. I assigned her code name, Esencia," she said. "She worked under me at MI6 until I announced my retirement. When I became managing partner at K19, she followed despite being offered a position with one of the most elite units of SIS."

"You feel responsible for her."

"I do. Beyond being one of the best agents I've ever worked with, Jaicon is a special person. There are things about her you should know. Things that would not be considered a betrayal of confidence."

"Go on." I took my arm from around her, and we walked several feet away from the others.

"She has a photographic memory."

"I am aware. We discussed it briefly."

"Did she mention her husband's accident?"

Husband? She was married? The foolishness I felt turned to shame. "She did not."

"Her husband was killed in an automobile accident three years ago. Jaicon was with him. He did not…pass right away."

The ramifications of Merrigan's words hit me so hard I grabbed her arm to steady myself. "My God," I whispered.

"The pain associated with the accident would be difficult for anyone to bear. For Jaicon, it's compounded."

"Yes. Of course. I understand."

I wanted to rush over to her, wrap her in my arms, and tell her how very sorry I was. But I had no right. When I looked up and our eyes met, I knew she sensed what Merrigan had just told me. I recognized the pain etched on her face—it was the same I felt when I thought about my Rosa.

"I fear what I'm about to say is none of my business," Merrigan said. "While Jaicon has not shared what might be between the two of you, I know her well enough to say you soothe her. Then again, you do that for everyone, don't you, Tryst?"

"You are right to think it is different with Jaicon."

Merrigan put her hand on my shoulder. "I say this with the deepest affection and caring."

I studied her.

"Be careful. For both your sakes."

I nodded slowly. "I appreciate your concern, my friend."

She embraced me, then left in search of Doc. Knowing Jaicon would be wondering about my reaction to the conversation her boss and I had had, I took a walk to think through what I'd learned.

Part of me wasn't surprised to hear she'd suffered a loss similar to the one I had. There were many instances when I sensed she understood far more about me than was said and vice versa. I'd attributed it to how easily we connected—forcing myself to stop short of going as far as to hint our souls recognized one another from past lives.

I'd heed Merrigan's warning, though. Neither of us had the capacity for great heartache. We'd already experienced too much of it in our lives.

While I didn't know how long Jaicon and her husband were together before his accident, time did not dictate the depth of emotion between two people. I'd spent a lifetime of love with my Rosa even though we were only given eighteen years together. I never dreamed that would be all we'd get. I expected to grow old together right here, on this ranch.

I couldn't imagine something similar with Jaicon, and if I were to pursue a romantic relationship with someone, I couldn't settle for anything less.

"What're you thinking about, Tryst?"

I raised my head and looked into my oldest nephew's eyes. "Hello, Brix. I didn't hear you approach."

"I noticed. That isn't like you. Is everything okay?"

I put my hand on his shoulder. "Contemplating the great mysteries of life. Or perhaps the injustices."

He studied me. "Why do I sense you aren't talking about the human trafficking victims who have been brought to the ranch?"

"My soul is heavy with sorrow over their plight, but you're right. There is more on my mind."

"Does it have anything to do with the pretty blonde woman who hasn't taken her eyes off you since I arrived?"

I followed his gaze to Jaicon, who turned away in the split second our eyes met.

"Who is she, Tryst? Or better put, who is she to you?"

I couldn't be untruthful nor could I be flippant. Which meant I had to think hard about my answer. Who was she to me? Someone who made me feel things I didn't think I'd ever feel again. Someone who, no matter the depth of our attraction, wasn't meant for me. More, I wasn't meant for her.

"She works for K19 Security Solutions and is here to aid with the victim reunification as well as to learn more about their abductors."

Brix raised a brow.

"She's a friend, nephew. No different than anyone else who visits the ranch."

He shook his head. "I know you wouldn't lie to me, which means you're lying to yourself."

In the weeks that followed, the majority of those rescued in Felixstowe returned to the lives they'd led before they were captured. Those remaining were refugees without homes or families to reunite with. They were given the option of returning to the country they'd left to journey into Mexico or to find gainful employment in Alamos. There was always work to be done on a ranch, and mine wasn't the only one in the area. The options for jobs were vast.

Between Jaicon, the rest of the team K19 had arranged to stay here, and myself, we were able to secure positions for all who wanted them.

A few took up their previous quest to seek asylum in the United States. We helped those individuals as much as we could, doing our best to counsel them not to put themselves at risk a second time. They thanked us but chose to try to get over the border anyway.

"You've done all you can, Tryst," Brix said the day I lamented the fate I feared awaited them. "You can't be responsible for everyone."

"I am aware."

He put his hand on my shoulder as I so often did to him. "I don't believe you are, and if you were honest with yourself, you'd admit it."

"Yes, nephew."

Brix laughed. "You sounded just like I did when I was a kid and my dad lectured me about something."

Alfonso Avila was my older brother by thirteen years. He passed away at the age of fifty-two from a massive heart attack. He was working alone in the vineyard at the time. We'd never know if he would've survived had he not been alone.

When it happened, I was here at the ranch. Rosa was two years into her cancer diagnosis and undergoing a combination of traditional and experimental treatment.

Alfonso's death hit me hard, but I hid my pain, not wanting it to affect my wife. I'd worried about Brix, his brothers, and his sister, knowing they would struggle to bring the harvest in that year without their father, but I couldn't leave Mexico, not with how precarious Rosa's health was then.

I didn't share my turmoil with Brix, then or now. However, between his father's death and my beloved's illness, I'd learned, in a very traumatic way, that I could not be responsible for everyone.

"Addison and I are leaving this afternoon. Are you sure you don't want to come with us and spend Thanksgiving with your family?"

"While I appreciate the invitation very much, as I told you when you asked previously, I cannot leave the ranch at this time."

I didn't need to follow my nephew's gaze to know who he saw. The way his eyes scrunched told me it was Jaicon.

"You know I want you to be happy."

I smiled. "Of course I do."

"Be careful."

It was the second time I'd received the warning, yet my intuition was telling me I'd be the one to hurt her rather than the other way around.

4

Jaicon

Tryst embraced his nephew Brix right before the man got in a nearby truck and drove away.

"Tomorrow is Thanksgiving," he said, walking over to stand by me as I contemplated whether I should visit the meditation center.

"I'd forgotten." It wasn't a holiday I'd ever celebrated in the UK. "Will you be traveling?"

Tryst shook his head. "We have several people from the States working on the ranch. I host a meal for those who choose to spend the day here."

"You're very kind to do so, especially given it will keep you from your family." There had been many instances when Tryst's depth of caring and compassion moved me. It seemed he erred on the side of selflessness every time.

"While I miss them very much, those who remain here are my people too."

Since arriving in Alamos, I'd learned a great deal about Tryst's family. Only some of the details were in his dossier.

His only sibling, a brother, had passed away the year before Tryst's wife died, leaving behind six sons and one daughter. The oldest son, Brix, owned the property adjacent to Tryst's ranch. He and his uncle were as close as father and son. While none of the others had visited over the last month, he spoke of them with the same deep affection.

It was during one such conversation that Tryst confided in me that he and his late wife had not had children of their own. He hadn't offered any reason why they didn't, and I refrained from asking. One, it was clear the topic made him uncomfortable. Two, it was none of my business. Three, if I had, he might've probed me on the subject.

"A new horse is arriving at the riding center today. Would you like to see her?"

"I'd love to." One of my favorite things about being here was having the chance to ride every day. It wasn't something I'd had time to do once I left home for university. The riding center Tryst referenced housed an equine rehabilitation program originally developed for people who had or were experiencing trauma. It grew to offer services for horses as well.

Tryst walked me to the *casita* where I changed into an appropriate attire. In case we had time to visit the meditation center later, as we did most days, I threw yoga pants and a T-shirt into a bag and brought it along.

"What's her story?" I asked on our way to the barns.

"She has suffered severe neglect and abuse. If you feel at all uncertain, we do not have to be there for her arrival."

"I can do it," I assured him.

Tryst had researched recent successes in helping those who suffered from a photographic memory. Essentially, the exercises involved working to replace negative memories with positive ones. By witnessing the horse's arrival, the idea was I'd gradually replace today's memory as she completed each step of her recovery. While certain recollections could never be erased, that I might have a tool to help eliminate some of the bad was promising.

"What is her name?" I asked when the truck pulling the trailer arrived.

"We weren't able to find out."

"Sad," I said under my breath.

Once one of the cowboys led her from the trailer, I witnessed the evidence of something far more heart-breaking than the animal not having a name. She was emaciated to the point where a clear outline of her rib cage was visible. There were also indications she'd been whipped.

When Tryst stepped closer, the animal's tail swished, she held her head high, her eyes were wide, and her ears were pinned. As I watched and listened to him soothe her, I recalled something I'd read on the subject of love.

While I remembered it word for word and could even visualize the pages of the book, I only focused on certain passages. Mainly on those saying love was a skill, not a feeling. It required trust, vulnerability, compassion, and generosity of the soul.

The article went on to say those who loved the best worked hard to give their life meaning and to find balance between their inner priorities and the demands of the outside world.

When I first read it, I was convinced no such person existed. However, I was looking at him. Tryst loved everyone and everything well. It was true of the human trafficking victims he'd nurtured and cared for, welcoming them on his ranch. It was true of the horse, who already showed signs of calming. And it was true of me too. The man had researched ways to help me navigate the difficulties of my memory. At any given time since I'd arrived, I felt him watching me, making sure I was not overly fatigued. When he did recognize something I needed—often before I realized it myself—he made it his business to ensure I got whatever it was. Even if it was venturing up a hillside to watch the sunset.

When he motioned to me, I walked over to him as he was still soothing the horse. I approached slowly and let her take her time sniffing my hand. When she raised her head, I rubbed her nose.

"She likes you," Tryst said, leaning into me. "She isn't the only one."

I smiled and shook my head like I always did when he flirted with me. "She needs a name."

"Have you thought of one?" Tryst asked.

"Have you?"

"Perhaps. Tell me yours first."

"Cariño."

His eyes scrunched, and he studied me long enough I felt self-conscious.

"What? Is that a bad name for a horse?"

Tryst shook his head. "It is the perfect name."

His reaction continued to trouble me even after we left the meditation center and he invited me to join him for dinner in the town of Alamos.

"What is on your mind, Jaicon?" he asked shortly after we drove out the ranch's gate.

I looked out the window rather than at him. "If there's something you don't like about the name I came up with for the horse, you certainly don't have to use it."

He reached over and rested his hand on mine. "I like it very much. I told you it was perfect."

Never did I believe Tryst was lying to me, including now. "There was something," I mumbled.

"Look at me, Jacy." He squeezed my fingers until I did. "It isn't the most obvious name—"

When I opened my mouth to speak, he squeezed harder.

"Most would probably say Dolly or Goldie or Bella or Honey. Yet, you thought of *Cariño*. The reason I reacted the way I did is because it was the very name I thought of right before you said it."

"Why do you think that is?"

He chuckled. "I fear you may not like my response."

"Tell me anyway."

"A soul tie."

I nodded. It's what I'd expected him to say, or something similar, simply because I felt it too.

He glanced over at me from time to time while keeping his eyes mainly on the road, but I didn't say anything. If he really believed we had such a connection, I didn't need to.

The following afternoon, Tryst served a grand Thanksgiving buffet. In addition to those staying, living, or working on *El Lugar de Curación*, he invited guests from neighboring ranches. I wouldn't be surprised to learn there were over one hundred people enjoying the feast he'd provided.

There were several appetizers, like roasted-pumpkin guacamole, green chile dip, and empanadas. Two kinds of turkey were served—one was cilantro-lime rubbed, and the other, a more traditional chorizo-stuffed. For those who didn't care for either, Tryst also provided pork tamales and sweet-potato–black-bean enchiladas.

Several side dishes were also served, including rice and beans, Mexican mashed potatoes, and roasted zucchini.

"I hope you saved room for dessert," he said, sitting beside me at one of the picnic tables.

I rubbed my stomach. "There is a chance I'll be hungry again in two or three days' time."

He held his hand out, and in it were two Mexican hot-chocolate cookies.

"Maybe just one." I plucked it from his palm.

"I was only offering one," he said, popping the second in his own mouth. "Can I interest you in a walk?"

"I desperately need one after all the food I consumed."

When Tryst took my hand and led me to the trail up the hillside where we often watched the setting sun, it felt like the most natural thing in the world.

"I had a really nice day. Thank you," I said once we reached the top.

"It is the best Thanksgiving I've had in a very long time." He brought my hand to his lips. "Thank you for sharing it with me."

"Tryst, I—"

He let go of my hand and put the tip of his index finger on my lips. "Shh. My apologies if I've gone too far."

He pulled away before I had the chance to tell him he hadn't. That I wished he'd gone further, and rather than kiss the back of my hand, I wished he'd kissed my lips.

I sighed. While I'd been using every excuse I could think of to remain here, perhaps it was time for me to leave the ranch.

"I've completed my report and need to move on to the next phase of my investigation."

He turned to face me rather than the view. "What do you mean?"

"I'll be traveling to the port where the first, and smaller, container raid took place."

"In Yavaros?"

"That's right."

"When will you return?"

"From there, I'll be heading to the Port of Altamira." It was where the ten shipping containers raided at the Port of Felixstowe had made their departure.

"Jaicon?"

"Yes?"

"You haven't answered my question."

"If you mean when will I return, I don't believe I will."

He studied me. "I must admit, I am somewhat surprised you didn't mention it until now."

"The reunification process is complete, as is my work here."

"I can be of assistance."

I raised a brow. "What do you mean?"

"I could go with you to Yavaros and to Altamira."

"Why?"

He smiled. "As I'm sure you recall, your colleagues at K19 staged their initial investigations from here. I was privy to the intelligence resulting in both raids."

"It isn't my decision. I'd have to talk it over with Doc and Merrigan."

He smiled again, and I laughed.

"You think they'll go along with your plan."

Tryst touched the tip of my nose with his finger. "I don't think; I know."

Tryst wasn't wrong. However, our departure to Yavaros was delayed when Merrigan said she and Doc were on their way to Alamos later that same day. When I asked why, she said she had a few things she wanted to discuss with me.

"How was your Thanksgiving?" she asked when Tryst and I met her and Kade after they pulled up near the main house.

"Abundant," I responded, winking.

"As are most things with Tryst. Even the intangible."

I completely agreed, particularly after he offered them wine and something to eat.

"I'll have a glass once Esencia and I have finished our conversation," Merrigan replied before turning to me. "Shall we?"

"What about Doc?" I asked when he didn't follow us to the *casita*.

"We've reviewed the things I plan to discuss with you."

I led her to the main room, and we each took a seat.

"Let's get right to it, yes?" she began.

"Please."

"As you are aware, the United Nations has formed a coalition intended to specifically address human trafficking, and five task forces, from the UK, US, Malta, Switzerland, and Albania, have been formed under the coalition."

"I've kept up with the briefings." I was also aware the coalition had recently raided a trafficking operation in Malta where a sex-slave auction was about to take place and that a civilian had shot and killed one of the men believed to have organized the abduction of at least twenty women, all of whom had been liberated.

"The UK task force suffered two casualties during the op in Malta."

"Yes." Jamie "Beak" Thomas and Tracy "Vulcan" North were both killed in the line of duty. I'd never worked a mission with either but had met both at SIS headquarters.

"Your name came up as a possible replacement."

I nodded. "It was in the brief."

"Before I ask if you're interested, I have another proposition for you."

"Go on."

"Last year, K19 Security Solutions added a new unit, Shadow Operations. Thus far, their missions have all been Stateside."

Shortly after the team's formation, they'd solved a decades-old serial killing investigation, resulting in the arrest and conviction of the man who'd masterminded the murders that took place over the course of fifty years.

"K19's founding partners have been exploring the possibility of adding another unit, one focused on international crime."

It made sense, given several people working for the firm served on the UN coalition's task forces.

"The proposed name is K19 Allied Intelligence, and I'm here to offer you the role of commander."

I rested against my chair, stunned. I'd anticipated the options she intended to discuss with me were to either serve on the UK task force, as she'd stated, or to be a member of this new team. "Commander?"

"Yes, Esencia."

"May I ask who else you're considering?"

"No one. In fact, unless you agree to head it up, we may reevaluate forming the unit."

"I wish I hadn't asked."

Merrigan smiled. "Yes, I'm sure knowing our intent makes your decision more difficult."

"I'm flattered."

"I'm sure you have questions."

The first I'd ask wasn't necessary information, but until I knew, I couldn't think of any others. "Where would the primary base of operation be located?"

She nodded in a way that led me to believe she'd anticipated the question. "Given the missions you'll be responsible for overseeing are international in nature, you could set up a command center, if you will, anywhere you'd like."

"Meaning in the UK or elsewhere in Eurasia?"

"Not necessarily. You could base it out of the US or even here, if you'd prefer."

"*Here?*" I gasped.

She smiled. "It was merely one suggestion."

"What of my current investigation?"

"It would continue on in the same manner it is now except instead of Doc or I determining what support is needed, you would."

"I see."

"You should be aware we've extended an offer to Tryst to serve as a consultant."

I wasn't surprised. "Has he accepted?"

"We asked he think it over, and we'd circle back to him at a later date."

"Is he aware of your offer to me?"

Merrigan leaned forward, and her eyes bored into mine. "No, Jaicon. The only people briefed on the new unit outside of Doc and me are Razor, Gunner, and Eighty-eight."

The men she mentioned, Tabon "Razor" Sharp, Gunner Godet, and Mercer "Eighty-eight" Bryant, were, along with Doc, the founding partners of the original K19.

"Would you like to discuss salary?" she asked.

"Of course."

"We're prepared to offer two hundred thousand US dollars. That is negotiable."

My eyes opened wide. "That's more than the chief of MI6 earns."

"Private intelligence is far more, shall we say, lucrative."

"How soon do you need my answer?"

"Take your time. As I said, nothing will change in regard to your current investigation. However, if you choose to accept, our next order of business will be to form a team to support the primary case the UN coalition is working on now."

"AMPS?"

"Correct."

The acronym was that of a shell corp whose assets were in Mauritian offshore accounts. One theory was each of the letters stood for the code name of the partners, who were believed to be big players in a human trafficking ring. Mithras, or M, was the man killed in Malta. The coalition was currently pursuing another suspect, *Pharaoh*. Thus far, no others had been identified.

Was the offer something I really needed to think about? Wasn't the role of commander something I'd aspired to? And while I earned a good salary as an independent contractor, I was paid per assignment.

"Are there benefits?"

"All the usual—paid leave, insurance, retirement." Merrigan's eyes opened wide. "You're seriously considering it, aren't you?"

Her hopeful expression faded when I shook my head, but just as quickly changed again when I said, "I've decided to accept."

5

Tryst

To my surprise, Kade and Merrigan returned to California the same day they arrived at my ranch. After Jaicon and I said our goodbyes, I sensed there was something on her mind she wasn't ready to confide in me. Rather than push, I asked if she'd like to join me to check how Cariño was adapting.

"I'd like that very much," she responded, but instead of looking at me, she appeared to be studying the horizon.

Rather than walk, I suggested we take the golf cart. The entire way, Jaicon surveyed the ranch as though it was the last time she'd see it. I took my hand from the wheel and brought it to my chest, rubbing the flesh above my aching heart. I wasn't ready to say farewell to this woman, yet I had nothing to offer to entice her to stay.

As I was parking the cart, one of the cowboys who worked with the equine rehabilitation program, Tex, came out of the barn. "How is the mare who arrived yesterday doing?" I asked, catching Jaicon's raised brow from the corner of my eye. "By the way, we named her Cariño," I added.

"Fittin' name," said Tex. "And she's doin' okay. One of the most skittish horses I've seen, but it's to be expected."

"How long do you plan to keep her in the barn?"

Tex shrugged. "I was thinking I'd bring her into the corral today. See what she does when she's got some room to move around."

"Would you be able to do so now?" Jaicon asked. It was the most engaged I'd seen her since before she and Merrigan went off on their own to chat.

Tex looked at me. "It's your decision."

"If it doesn't interfere with your plans, then by all means."

"Fine by me. Give me a minute to get the other horses into the pasture, then I'll bring her out."

We walked over to the split-rail fence and waited.

"Jaicon, I—" I began at the same time she said my name.

"Go ahead," she said.

"No, please, you go first."

She sighed, and her eyes scrunched. "You're probably wondering about my meeting."

"I will admit I'm curious."

"While it won't change my immediate plans, I've been offered a new position with K19."

"I see."

"Do you?"

I smiled. "I do not, actually."

"I asked Merrigan if she told you."

"And?"

"She said she hadn't. I know better than to think she'd lie."

I put my hand on her shoulder. "You're feeling unsettled."

She nodded, and her eyes bored into mine. "You do that to me, Tryst. And before you do, it isn't something I want you to apologize for."

Rather than hesitate, like I had every time I felt the urge to hug her, I pulled her into my arms. "You unsettle me too, Jacy."

Too soon, she took a step back, out of my arms, and while I momentarily considered saying I was sorry for overstepping, I stopped myself.

"I'll be heading up a new unit for them. One focused on international investigations."

While I did everything in my power to mask my reaction, I felt deflated. "When does this take effect?"

"Immediately, I suppose. As I said, I'll be continuing with my current case since it's international in nature. This does involve you, at least in part."

Like I did my best to mask my disappointment earlier, now I tried not to appear too hopeful.

"Merrigan mentioned they extended an offer to you to serve as a consultant."

"That is true."

"She also said she asked you to think it over. In all fairness, before you make your decision, you should know you'd be working with me. At least for the time being. If you'd prefer not to—"

"I'd prefer to only work with you."

Jaicon smiled. "You may quickly change your mind."

"Never."

"Look! There she is," Jaicon said, pointing as Tex led Cariño out of the barn. "It's heartbreaking. How could someone hurt an animal in such a way?" she muttered.

"We will do everything in our power to help her heal." We watched Tex release the catch rope, then take two steps away. Cariño didn't move other than to swish her tail, raise her head, and hollow her back.

Tex took several more steps away, eventually coming to the fence a few feet from where we stood, watching. He climbed up and sat on the top rail.

The horse stayed motionless for several minutes, then dropped her head and slowly walked around the corral.

"This is a good sign," I murmured.

"We're starting her off slow with small amounts of high-quality alfalfa and makin' sure she takes in enough water," said Tex, never taking his eyes off the animal. "She's still spooked and probably will be for some time."

The three of us watched the horse make her way around the outer edges of the enclosed area. Once she was within a few feet of us, I anticipated her turning and going across rather than walking too close. Instead, she stopped near Jaicon. Her ears remained pinned, her head high, but her eyes didn't seem to dart around as much.

When she held out her hand, Cariño didn't flinch. Jaicon eased over, keeping her arm extended, and eventually rubbed her nose. When the time came for the beguiling woman to leave, I predicted the horse and I would miss her equally.

"I'm sorry. I have to answer this," she said, walking away when her phone vibrated.

"Can I take her back in, boss?" Tex asked.

"Yes, let's not overtire her."

I climbed up on the fence and sat, looking beyond the corral to the pasture. There was nowhere on earth I loved being as much as this. The sound of leaves quaking in the breeze, the distant neighing of horses, and the gurgling stream that was closer to a trickle this time of year were all sounds that soothed me.

While I missed Rosa every day, I rarely felt lonely. Just the idea that Jaicon might leave made me feel isolated. These new emotions perplexed me.

"That was an update from Ares. You met him, yes?" said Jaicon, walking over to the fence.

I hopped down. "Not met, but I do know who you're talking about."

"As I said previously, twice actually, everything is status quo as far as my trip to Yavaros and Altamira."

Her trip. Not *our* trip. I waited for her to continue.

Jaicon's eyes scrunched. "We didn't finish our earlier conversation. You were still thinking over whether you'd be interested in consulting."

"I've made my decision."

She half smiled.

"I am interested."

"I'm so pleased, Tryst. And, from what I understand, you have some experience."

I shook my head. "Experience? No. None at all. I am but a lowly rancher."

"Right. It's all an urban legend, then?"

"What is?" I winked. Of course she was referring to Los Caballeros. I didn't kid myself about the organization started by my grandfather's ancestors. While we operated in relative anonymity, our "secret" society hadn't been so in many years. Particularly to someone like a former MI6 agent.

Before leaving for Yavaros, there was another matter Jaicon and I needed to address. If I was to serve as a consultant to K19, I'd need to know where she planned to set up her main base of operation. While I often traveled to California, being gone for any extended period of time meant I should meet with the managers of the ranch as well as the equine rehabilitation program.

"There's been a slight change in our itinerary," she said, looking at her phone. "Ares sent an updated brief regarding what we're referring to as the AMPS mission. Merrigan is requesting we travel to California rather than Yavaros or Altamira."

"What can I do to assist?" I asked.

"Nothing I can think of immediately. While she didn't specifically say, my guess is we'll be there overnight, at least."

"What about scheduling a flight?"

"Doc has arranged for a plane to pick us up."

I raised a brow. "Just the two of us?"

"It's a small aircraft—a Cirrus SF50 Vision Jet. They're quite nice, with the added benefit of not needing a copilot."

I was aware of the model she mentioned. While not a pilot myself, I flew in private planes enough to appreciate something as nice as the Vision. Then again, it came with a two-million-dollar price tag.

"One of the best things about it is how almost all the preflight checks are automated. Well, that and the visibility. Besides the F-22 Raptor, the Vision is my favorite plane to fly."

"I had no idea you were a pilot," I said.

"Former RAF. I flew F-15s as well."

I shook my head in amazement. The woman was a marvel. The more I learned about her, the more she excited me.

The force of my desire for her was so powerful, it was all I could do not to walk up behind her, wrap my arms around her waist, and kiss my way from one side of her neck to the other. I closed my eyes and imagined sweeping her into my arms, carrying her into my house, and spending hours making slow, sweet love to her. If only she were mine.

"Tryst?"

I opened my eyes to find Jaicon standing close enough for me to reach out and touch her. I raised my arm, but dropped it. "My apologies. There's something I must take care of at the barn."

"Don't," she said when I turned my back to her.

"I'm sorry?" I said, glancing over my shoulder.

"Soul ties," she murmured. "They're powerful between us."

I turned to face her. "They are, and sometimes…"

"What?"

"I find the connection difficult to deny."

She took two steps closer. "Does it have to be denied?"

"I'm sorry, but it does."

"Tryst?" she repeated as I walked away. This time, I didn't respond.

6

Jaicon

I felt like such a bloody fool. I'd come close to throwing myself at Tryst—seducing him. Thank God I hadn't stuck my foot deeper into it. Even what little I had done made the man so uncomfortable he'd left my presence.

The concept of soul ties was one I'd read about in the months after my husband died. Then, it had been in an effort to break one.

Essentially, the phrase referred to an emotional and spiritual connection between two people—a bond that *could* be strong and long-lasting. It could also be unhealthy, particularly in a case similar to mine.

I was twenty-nine when an accident took my husband's life. I was left with a sense of emptiness, a fear my life lacked meaning without him. There were days when I wondered if I had reason to go on. I felt anxious on my own. I struggled with making decisions, given I was so used to getting his input. It grew to the point where I couldn't define my identity without him. The worst, though, was the sense of emptiness I felt from the moment I woke in the morning until exhaustion finally overtook me and I slept.

At the time, flying became the only thing I had where I could make decisions on my own. In order to operate an aircraft, I had to constantly be aware of my surroundings and those of the plane.

While my husband had been with MI6, his career trajectory was very different than mine. He hadn't been with the RAF and had never flown any kind of aircraft. Thus, he'd never once been in the cockpit with me. I was already used to that kind of solitude.

"Wow," said Tryst, approaching me as I reviewed the flight plan with the pilot who'd flown the Vision from California and landed it on the ranch's private runway.

"She's a beauty," I said, motioning to it.

"She certainly is," said Tryst, not taking his eyes from mine.

I opened the single door on the left side of the plane. The bifold design revealed a good-sized entry area.

"Go ahead," the pilot said, motioning for me to take the captain's seat.

I ran my hands over the supple leather and got situated. The jet had a lot of head and shoulder room and a windscreen that was divided in the middle. The forward visibility was amazing, while the side view was nothing short of spectacular.

The avionics suite featured two big fourteen-inch displays up front, while a step below were three touch-controller displays that had been mounted sideways.

"Amazing," I commented, pointing to the side-sticks on the left and right that traveled fore and aft like a more conventional yoke.

I initiated the start sequence and watched as the system ran its own series of checks on everything from TAWS to fire suppression. I moved the dial from the OFF position to RUN, and the single engine started itself.

Once we were in the air, I wished Tryst was seated beside me instead of the other pilot, mainly because it wasn't necessary for him to be supervising me. This plane was rated for a single flier, and I didn't like anyone looking over my shoulder, so to speak. When he made the third *suggestion* about something he thought I should be doing, I turned to him. "Would you mind switching with the gentleman seated in the cabin?" I asked in my sugary-sweetest tone of voice, given if I hadn't, I might've snapped at him.

"Yes, ma'am," he said, unfastening his seat belt.

I breathed a sigh of relief when Tryst took the other seat.

"I wondered how long you'd last," he said, leaning close enough for me to hear him whisper.

"I was about to belt him," I whispered back.

Tryst laughed out loud. "I do enjoy your company, Jaicon."

"Likewise."

The rest of the flight was so much nicer. Rather than telling me how to control the plane, Tryst marveled at the amazing view afforded by the aircraft's design.

I was enjoying flying so much, I was disappointed when I realized how close we were to the airfield outside Montecito. However, given Merrigan intended for us to have continued to use of the Vision, I didn't suggest going farther and circling back.

"I'd forgotten how inviting Kade's place is," said Tryst when he pulled up to the gate in the SUV that had been parked in the Vision's hangar and that Merrigan had indicated was for our use.

"Have you visited before?"

"Kade and I have been friends since we were kids."

I raised a brow.

"I am three years his senior."

I hadn't thought about their proximity in age, but it made sense now that I did.

We drove through when the gate opened, and pulled up to the front door, where Doc and Merrigan waited.

"How was the flight?" she asked as we cheek-kissed.

I smiled. "A dream."

"I knew you'd enjoy it."

I looked over at the house. "This is lovely."

"I'd say thank you, but this is all Kade."

The Spanish-style building's exterior was white stucco with dark-brown shutters and a red-tile roof. Massive palm trees stretched high above the roofline, and bright-pink bougainvillea grew everywhere I looked. Big urns overflowing with flowers flanked the front door.

"Would you like to come in or follow the boys to the garage?" she asked. "Kade acquired a new vehicle yesterday, and he's anxious to show off. I'm afraid I wasn't effusive enough when he presented it to me."

I laughed. "I'd be the same way. Now, if it was a plane…"

She laughed like I had.

"Oh, how nice," I said, motioning to the massive fireplace in the room just off the foyer.

"We keep it lit at this time of year. It gets quite chilly this close to the ocean."

Everything in the room matched the size of the stone enclosure where logs burned. Behemoth wood beams adorned the vaulted ceilings, and the furniture in the room was all oversized. While mostly covered by woven New Mexican rugs, the pavers underneath were the biggest I'd ever seen.

"Can I get you anything to eat?"

"Perhaps just a beverage," I said, following her into the kitchen. "Where are Laird and Rielle?" I asked.

"With their grandparents. They begged us to stay with them after the holiday."

"How old are they now?"

"Laird is three, and Rielle is two. It seems just yesterday they were both babies."

She pulled a bottle of wine from the refrigerator and held it up.

"Yes, please."

After pouring two glasses, she motioned to the dining table where her laptop sat. It was just off the open-plan kitchen. "We'll get started as soon as Kade and Tryst come inside. By the way, before I forget, his security clearance was upgraded this morning, not that I doubted it would be."

I nodded, wondering why I hadn't thought to initiate it. Perhaps Merrigan should reconsider offering me the position of commander.

"How are you, Jaicon?" she asked when we took a seat.

"Honestly, I've no idea."

"My guess is Tryst would respond in a similar way."

Before I could say anything further, the two men joined us.

"While Esencia has received regular briefings, I thought we'd bring Tryst up to speed on the investigations K19 Allied Intelligence will be supporting,"

Merrigan began, handing a file to the three of us before opening her own.

I flipped to the first page, which was an overview of the two ops Tryst was already aware of. However, his security clearance had been increased from secret to top secret, which meant there was information contained in the brief he hadn't previously been privy to.

Doc cleared his throat. "To review, on 18 October, a woman with a personal connection to someone with K19 Security Solutions, Luisa Reeve, was abducted in San Luis Obispo, California. A week later, on 25 October, acting on an informant's tip, a K19 team raided a container at the Port of Yavaros destined for Yangshan Port in Shanghai, China. During that op, one victim was killed along with four suspected human traffickers. Three others were apprehended. After being interrogated, they were taken into federal custody. The ringleader and man who had originally abducted Ms. Reeve, Manual Varilla, had several outstanding warrants for trafficking, resulting in him turning state's evidence.

"Varilla claimed Reeve was not in Yavaros, as we believed. Rather, she had been transported to the Port of Altamira on the Gulf of Mexico, where she was one of an indeterminate number of victims held captive in shipping containers loaded onto a vessel bound for the Port of Felixstowe."

Doc turned to the next page. "There, a joint coalition made up of K19, MI6, and the US and UK immigration services raided the vessel and liberated one hundred and eighty-five victims out of ten different containers."

He looked up from the document. "An important side note. On the floor of one of the containers, the word 'Mithras' was scrawled in the dirt." Doc turned and looked from me to Tryst. "Any questions thus far?"

"Negative," I responded. Tryst shook his head.

"Unfortunately, there were no suspects traveling in the containers. Thus, other than the dockmaster, who had altered the manifest to indicate the ship was arriving ten hours later than it had, no other arrests were made."

From the corner of my eye, I saw Tryst nod in understanding. That was one of the points of information he hadn't known previously.

"Teams were dispatched to the locations listed on the authentic manifest for delivery of the containers; however, in every case, the destination was an abandoned warehouse."

"Pardon my interruption," said Merrigan, "but it should also be noted that Operation Felixstowe was the second official mission conducted by the five task forces making up the UN Coalition Against Human Trafficking."

Doc continued. "The first, Operation Purfleet, was led by former members of MI5. A team of agents tracked two other containers that had arrived at the port the op was named for. Tragically, one hundred and twenty-four victims were found deceased when the rigs hauling the containers stopped at an industrial complex not far from the port, and the agents initiated the raid."

Doc ran his hand over his bald head. I'd realized, some time ago, it was something he did when he was forced to brief a team on something he wished he wasn't. He cleared his throat and continued.

"Through the combined efforts of the five task forces, that particular op led to the deployment of separate raids, taking place in the same twenty-four-hour period, during which two major trafficking crime rings, one in Lesovo, Bulgaria, and the other in Edirne,

Turkey, were taken down. Upwards of sixteen hundred people were rescued that day, and countless arrests were made."

Doc turned to Merrigan, and she nodded. "It was during Operation Purfleet that Margeaux 'Nemesis' Jordan, then the UK task force commander, made contact with another former MI6 agent, Jennifer "Oleander" Smith." She looked over at me. "Were you and O slated to move into Unit 23 at the same time?"

"We were."

She put her hand on mine. "I'm so very glad you chose us instead."

"What is Unit 23?" Tryst asked.

"It's the most covert of SIS' ultra-secretive entities," Merrigan explained. "It's made up of former SAS—Special Air Service—like Jaicon was. The unit is quite…formidable."

I didn't turn to look at Tryst, but I could feel his eyes on me. Was he aware one of the primary mandates of the unit was the assassination of known terrorists and other enemies of the Crown?

Kade returned to the brief. "Through Oleander, we learned of Mithras, the first suspect in what we believe is one of the largest trafficking rings in the world. They allegedly operate out of Egypt, Iraq, Syria, and Turkey, running both a high-end sex trade as well as mid-level slave labor and trafficking for prostitution."

He flipped to the next page. "Fast forward to 12 November of this year. Mithras was identified as Lorenzo Moretti, who was believed to be behind an auction site on the dark web where someone known to a member of the UK team was offered for bid. Investigations led to the discovery of the IP address' origin. On 15 November, a raid was deployed at that location on the Maltese island of Gozo. Nineteen women were rescued prior to the start of the auction. In a separate incident, on 20 November, Mithras, who was about to be arrested, was shot and killed by a civilian."

I glanced over and saw Tryst had been taking notes while Doc spoke.

"That brings us to today. Concurrent to that op, a team comprised of Oleander, Wren Alexander-Whittaker, Hanadarko Hunter, and a new MI5 hire, Bexli Everdeen, came up with a lead into the possible identity of a second suspect believed to be working with Mithras."

"Did you say Bexli Everdeen?" Tryst asked, flipping to a previous page.

"Yes," Merrigan responded. "Mithras abducted her and took her to Malta. Unbeknownst to him, she snapped a mobile photo of him with a woman. That woman was working at the US Embassy in Malta and was believed to be a mole."

"It was Bexli who determined 'Pharaoh' was a woman, not a man as we'd previously believed," Doc added.

Tryst tapped the paper with the eraser end of the pencil he held.

"What are you thinking?" I asked. Before he could respond, Doc's, Merrigan's, and my mobile vibrated.

"Dammit," Doc muttered.

I turned to Tryst. "Two victims who were at the ranch were found dead near La Higuera." Like I assumed Doc felt earlier, having to tell Tryst the details was difficult. "They were shot execution-style."

Tryst put his head in his hands, covering his face. I had no doubt it was in an effort to hide his devastation. "They didn't make it one hundred miles."

I put my hand on his arm. "We both did everything we could to discourage them from leaving the ranch on their own." Something else occurred to me. "You said two."

"That's right," Doc responded.

I turned to Tryst. "Five men left together that day. Not two."

"You are correct."

"Looks like we've got ourselves a murder suspect—or three," said Doc, rubbing his hands together.

When I noticed he and Merrigan were once again studying their mobiles, I looked at mine. Our eyes met when I finished reading.

"What is it? Tryst asked.

"Mexican authorities were able to identify the two men via their fingerprints. Both had warrants for their arrest," Merrigan told him.

None of the victims rescued from the shipping containers were carrying any kind of ID. Given the number of refugees, it had been a challenge to identify some of the people. However, given the horrifying ordeal they'd been through, we'd accepted what they told us and didn't treat them like criminals.

"What were the warrants for?"

"Trafficking," said Doc. "And it gets even more complicated; there's an alleged connection to Manual Varilla.

During the next hour, several things happened. First, Merrigan initiated a videoconference with the coalition leader, Nemesis, as well as each of the task force commanders—Philip "Ares" Kappas from the US, Winston "Cayman" Trace from the UK, Kai "Poseidon" Allora from Malta, Henry "Zeppelin" Bonham, a former member of MI6 who was tapped to lead the Swiss team, and finally, Justin "Magnet" Magnussen, who like Zep was former MI6 but had been appointed to lead the Albanian unit.

"Jesus, we were wrong about no guards being in the containers," said Ares after Doc briefed them on the information we'd just received. It was evident he was feeling as though he'd misread the situation on the ground at Felixstowe. However, as Doc reminded him, he wasn't alone in his assessment. Every agent who'd participated in the raid believed as Ares had.

"The reunification process is complete, yes?" Nemesis asked.

"Affirmative," I confirmed.

"What do you suggest?" Merrigan asked, turning to me.

"We'll need to reassemble as many of the original team members as possible, along with whoever else you can spare from the Pharaoh op," I said, looking at each of the task force commanders.

"Ares?" prompted Nemesis.

He'd been typing something on his laptop. "Tank, Blackjack, and Atticus are available."

"How quickly can they deploy?" I asked.

"They'll be on the next flight out," said Ares. "Doc, you got any favors you can call in for transport?"

"Roger that. I'll have a plane waiting at Gatwick this afternoon."

"Anything else we need to cover now?" Merrigan asked.

"The most urgent of our tasks is reassembling the team in Alamos." I turned to Tryst. "With your permission, of course."

"Permission granted."

7

Tryst

Doc and Merrigan invited us to spend the night in their home since the teams would not arrive at my ranch for two or three days. Having dinner with them felt like we were two couples on a double date rather than colleagues. A number of times, I thought about reaching over to hold Jaicon's hand the same way Kade held Merrigan's.

When it came time to go to bed, I longed to follow her into the guest room Merrigan had directed her to and sleep with her in my arms.

While I was tired, it took me some time to fall asleep as I lay in bed, fantasizing about the woman who captivated me endlessly.

Her smile, her laughter, and even the way she brought a glass of wine to her mouth, first breathing in its aroma, then taking a sip of the delectable beverage, all left me breathless.

I imagined the noises of pleasure she'd made as she lingered over the taste would be similar to those we would both make when I licked through her folds, savoring her taste like I did the wine. I fought against getting up, going to the room next door where I knew she slept, and climbing in bed, next to her.

In my fantasies, I'd find her naked. She'd turn her body toward mine and tell me how she'd hoped I'd come to her. I would take her lips, kissing her like I'd longed to since the first moment I met her. Jaicon would be needy. She'd demand I remove the boxers I slept in, and when I had, she'd wrap her hand around my hardness and spread her legs, begging for my touch.

As much as I'd want to enjoy how good it felt to have her stroke me, I'd remove her hand from my cock and shift my body so I rested between her legs. She'd beg to feel me inside her, but I'd force her to wait. First, I'd bring her pleasure with my mouth and fingers. After making her come again and again, I'd finally ease my steel-hard cock into her wetness. I wouldn't rush, no matter how much she pleaded. I'd take my time, driving her to the point of a desire so profound that when

I finally allowed her to orgasm, she'd scream out my name at the same time I did hers.

I used my own hand to release the sexual tension that would not allow me to sleep. I came hard, picturing Jaicon in the other room, doing the same thing.

When my gaze met hers the next morning at breakfast and she smiled, her eyes drooping, her mouth pouty, I was transported right back to the fantasy, wondering if she had thought about me while lying in bed alone.

"Good morning, Jaicon. How did you sleep?" I asked, wishing I could cup her cheek and offer my morning salutation with a kiss.

"Not that well. You?"

I half smiled and shook my head. "My mind would not let me rest. My body would not, either."

Her eyes bored into mine. Was she wondering what I meant, or was her restlessness caused by the same thing mine was?

"We'll be returning to your ranch today. I filed a flight plan for thirteen hundred hours. Do I need to delay for any reason?" she asked.

"I travel at your convenience," I said, winking.

Jaicon smiled. "I was thinking of walking on the beach. Are you interested in joining me?"

"I would enjoy doing so very much."

"How are you feeling about yesterday afternoon's news?" she asked once we arrived at the oceanfront park named for Esther Hammond, a philanthropist who'd owned forty-six acres of shoreline in the early nineteen hundreds. Upon her death, the land was given to the people of California and turned into a state park.

"I am troubled, as I'm sure you are. That the very people responsible for the horrors the innocent endured traveled among them, stayed at the ranch with them, is very worrisome. I am thankful nothing else happened while, at the same time, curious about the other three men who set out with the two who are now deceased. Were they traffickers as well or victims?"

"Both are possibilities. That there were other imposters in the containers with the victims is part of what kept me awake last night. If there were, they slipped right through our hands."

A part of me wanted to ask what else had, but with the seriousness of her words, I could not be so flippant. "Making that determination will be difficult," I said instead.

"Impossible."

Unable to stop myself, I put my arm around her shoulders. "As Doc reminded Ares, many other intelligence professionals made the same determination—that the victims had been locked in the containers with no means of escape, therefore unguarded."

"The two men executed in La Higuera likely knew there *was* a way out. If there were other traffickers pretending to be victims, they likely did too. They would've saved themselves with no regard for the lives of the rest. Not that they believed those lives had value other than the money they'd make from enslaving them."

"They were found dead in La Higuera and shot execution-style. I believe both points of information are significant," I said.

"I agree, but I am interested in hearing your theory."

"They were being watched, and the people doing it were familiar with the ranch's security systems."

"Which means they were already on the inside."

"Precisely. Had they not been, we would've picked up on their presence."

"Which also means they had to be among the last to leave. Or left with them."

I nodded in agreement. "Perhaps informing Manual Varilla of the deaths of men with a connection to him would lead to information regarding their killers."

"Excellent idea. Unless he's been relocated, he is in Pelican Bay State Prison in Crescent City. Once we file the flight plan and are in the air, we can be there in a little under two hours. I'll talk with Merrigan about how best to arrange a visit with him."

"How may I be of help?" I asked.

"I'll need to talk with Merrigan before I file with the FAA."

"As much as I hate to cut our walk short, we should return to the house," I suggested.

Kade was able to contact the warden at Pelican Bay and arranged for Jaicon and me to meet with Varilla later that afternoon. As Jaicon said, the flight to the Crescent City airfield took less than two hours. Either he or Merrigan had scheduled a car and driver to meet us on the tarmac and deliver us to the prison. The same driver took us back to the plane at the conclusion of the meeting that hadn't garnered the results I hoped it would. Jaicon, though, wasn't as disheartened.

"What happens next will tell us more than Manual would have anyway," she said.

"Do you believe he'll orchestrate retaliation from his prison cell?"

"I do. However, it may take some time for us to find those retaliated against."

We spent one more night at Kade and Merrigan's in Montecito, then returned to the ranch the following day. By the time we arrived, Tank, Blackjack, and Atticus were already there.

Gehring "Mantis" Cassman and his wife, Manon "Alegria" Cassman, were on their way. They were two of the pilots who'd transported victims from Felixstowe to Alamos. Tabon "Razor" Sharp, Gunner Godet, Thomas "Dutch" Miller, and his wife, Malin

Miller, were arriving with them. The four had assisted with the reunification process.

The ten of us spent the next two weeks reviewing photos of the victims as well as pouring over the information gathered about them. Those we identified as potential suspects were divvied up among teams for further investigation.

None of our leads panned out, which wasn't a surprise. Investigations could take days, weeks, months, even years before a single puzzle piece could bring it all together.

While we were both busy following up on every bit of intel we received, Jaicon and I fell back into the routine of visiting the barns and the meditation center every chance we could. The recurring fantasies I had about her, that began in Montecito, continued to plague me. I longed for her in a way I didn't recall ever feeling before, even for my Rosa.

Today, Jaicon and I were leaning against the fence of the corral, watching Tex work with Cariño. As it did so often, the occasional brush of her arm against mine sent jolts of desire through me. However, I couldn't allow myself to pull her close or breathe in her scent. If

I did any of those things, I doubted I'd be able to stop myself from kissing her. Every time she spoke, I found myself studying her lips rather than paying attention to her words. She'd called me out on it a few times. While we both laughed, I worried how uncomfortable my obvious desire made her.

Jaicon's nonverbal cues were inconsistent, something that could be attributed to the serious nature of the work we did each day, or she could be struggling to handle the powerful attraction between us in the same way I was. While my Rosa had been gone for many years, at times the thoughts I had about Jaicon felt adulterous. Perhaps she felt the same way.

My phone vibrated with a text message from Brix. It was a photo taken from high above the ranch. When I looked up, I saw him waving from the hilltop.

Need to run something by you, the following message said. *Would now be a good time?*

Of course, I responded. *I'll come to you.*

I excused myself and told Jaicon I'd catch up with her later. Rather than take the golf cart, I walked beyond the meditation center and took the trail that led to the ranchland I'd deeded Brix and his wife as an early wedding gift.

We embraced like we always did, even when it had only been a few hours since we were last together.

"How are you, nephew?" I asked.

"To be honest, I never realized life could be this good."

"It warms my heart to hear you say so."

"Another of the *caballeros* has found the woman of his dreams."

"Wonderful!" I exclaimed, having no doubt he spoke of his closest friend.

"Ridge and Seraphina are getting married."

"Again, fantastic news." Seraphina was sister to Luisa Reeve, one of the women rescued in Felixstowe. She and Noah—who everyone, including Brix, called Ridge—met when she asked Los Caballeros to help find the missing woman. Knowing the task was beyond our ability, I went to Doc and Merrigan, who mobilized K19 to stage the mission. Throughout the rescue process and afterward, it had been clear to me Ridge and his betrothed were falling in love. It took them slightly longer to realize it themselves.

"Have they set a date?" I asked.

"They have. Christmas, and they'd like to hold the ceremony here at the ranch, in the chapel."

The chapel, or temple, Brix spoke of was one of the most magical places on the property. It hadn't yet been built when Rosa and I married. In fact, this would be the first wedding to take place there. My heart was overjoyed that one finally would. "It will be an honor to host such an important occasion."

"You know Christmas is only a couple of weeks away, right?"

I smiled and nodded. "They will have a wedding fit for a prince and princess. I promise."

"I don't doubt it, Tryst, and thank you."

8

Jaicon

While security on the ranch was tight, extremely so for a property such as this, some holes still concerned me. Since Tryst was busy getting everything in place for the wedding, Tank and I focused on determining how many additional team members would be needed the week leading up to the event.

At our request, K19 Security Solutions arranged for several operatives to be here for support, to the point where, quite honestly, we were buttoned-up tighter than many of the royal weddings I'd worked early in my career.

By the time the bride, groom, and their families arrived from California via a private aircraft and landed on the ranch's airstrip, all strategic elements were ready for their safety.

Something, though, was bothering me. I checked and double-checked the action plan and found nothing out of place. Still, the niggling feeling wouldn't go away.

While the wedding was happening, I found out why.

"This couldn't be worse timing," said Ares, calling after the ceremony had gotten underway. "Poseidon and Oleander found another auction site."

"And?"

"Luisa Reeve is on it. It appears a bidding war turned into a bounty shortly after her rescue in Felixstowe. The current price on her head is a quarter of a million US dollars."

My stomach lurched.

"We need a twenty on Luisa Reeve," I said, covering my mobile's mic with my hand. Blackjack and Atticus took off from the *casita* that served as our command center while Tank and I continued to monitor the cameras and other hotspots around the ranch.

"I'm not comfortable with her remaining at this location," I said to Ares.

"The plane is still there, right?"

"Affirmative," I responded.

"Let's relocate her as soon as possible."

"I agree. I'll work on a flight plan now."

"I'm not sure whether you've been briefed, but Beau Barrett along with Snapper and Kick Avila have been consulting with us from California."

"I am aware." The three men had been hired to look into the other players involved in Luisa Reeve's abduction as well as to see what they could find out about the trafficking rings operating out of the San Luis Obispo area. As locals, they'd been able to cultivate sources far more easily than we could.

"I'll make direct contact with Beau. I'd like him to remain on the ranch for the time being, at least until the rest of the guests return to the States," said Ares. "Doc and Merrigan have made arrangements to transport Tank, Blackjack, and Atticus to wherever you are as soon as you've made a determination."

"Roger that."

"Also, Zeppelin and Magnet are traveling to the States now. As soon as you can, advise me of your destination. They're due to land in San Francisco in the next hour. One more thing, I'd like to arrange for the profilers to speak with Luisa."

"Ares, please understand I mean no disrespect when I say I'm not sure she is emotionally capable of doing so presently."

"Mayhem and Hanadarko are pros."

While I couldn't speak for Hanadarko, since I'd never met the woman, let alone worked with her, Mayhem could be abrasive.

"I'd like to at least try."

"I will speak with her."

"Thanks, Esencia."

Thirty minutes later, I left the surveillance room, stepped out of the *casita*, and came face-to-face with Tryst.

"Is it true?" he asked.

"I fear it is. The best option is to get Luisa removed from the property posthaste."

"Press Barrett is making arrangements now."

"I should travel with them. However, I don't want to increase Luisa's level of stress."

"The solution is an easy one. You are a pilot. By going with them, you can be in the cockpit with Zin."

"Of course," I said, nodding. "I should get with Press on the flight plan. I intended to file it myself, but he needs to, as the aircraft's owner."

Tryst stepped closer. Our eyes met, and in them, I saw the same warmth and affection I always did. While nothing romantic had occurred between us, whenever we were together, the air around us felt electrically charged.

If only our stars had aligned differently. If we both hadn't lost the two people we believed were the loves of our lives. If we were closer in age. If I wasn't the commander of a unit for what was now the largest private security and intelligence firm in the world. And if only he didn't live on a ranch in Mexico, where he ran a rehabilitation center so near to his heart. There were simply too many "if onlys" for us to consider acting on our mutual attraction.

I knew Tryst felt it as strongly as I did and struggled with it too.

"Jaicon," he whispered, cupping my cheek with his palm.

Had I ever experienced a touch that felt so perfect? I couldn't stop myself from leaning into his hand.

"I know this is unfair of me to say, but being away from you…"

"I feel the same."

"Jacy, I want to kiss you."

"I want you to."

He angled my face and touched his lips to mine. It felt so right yet so wrong at the same time. It had been years since I'd kissed anyone other than my husband. When Tryst coaxed my lips apart and touched the tip of his tongue to mine, I pulled back. I wasn't ready for this.

"Please, Jaicon, let me know the softness of your mouth, your taste."

I answered with my tongue, swirling it with his when he kissed me again. Bringing my hands up, I dug my fingers into the flesh on his shoulders and angled my body so I could press against him. When I felt his hardness nestle between my legs, I was jolted out of the momentary spell I was under and pushed away.

"Tryst, I…I need to go," I said, wishing with everything inside me I didn't have to, but knowing it was for the best.

"Jacy—"

I shook my head. "Let me go, Tryst."

"I understand." He nodded solemnly, almost as if in prayer.

I rushed off in search of Press, who I found coming out of Tryst's house.

"We've decided to go to Napa. There are guesthouses on my parents' estate, and the security was designed by Burns Butler."

"Copy that," I said, already aware of the systems in place both at Press' parents' residences and at his own.

"We're ready to leave whenever you are," he added.

I was in the plane's main cabin with Luisa Reeve until we reached cruising altitude, then I joined Zin in the cockpit so Press could be with her. When it came time for our descent, I returned.

"How are you holding up?" I asked, sitting in the seat beside Luisa.

She shrugged. "Okay. Thanks."

"Press mentioned he informed you of the reason we left Mexico. If you have any questions or concerns, I'm available at any time."

"Thanks, Jaicon."

"And please, call me Jacy."

"Again, thank you, Jacy. So, um, Press said you used to work for MI6."

"I did."

"Do you miss it?"

"What I do now isn't terribly different. I once hoped to work with Fatale. You probably know her as Merrigan. Anyway, I expected she'd take over as chief.

When she passed on the job, I was quite disappointed, to be honest. Working with her now makes up for it."

"Wait, I remember Merrigan saying she left MI6 a few years ago."

I cocked my head. "Yes."

"A *few* years ago, I was still in high school. You don't appear to be much older than me."

"Thank you, but if that's the case, I'm considerably older than you are." I smiled. "I do hear that quite often. I've my mother to thank for my youthful appearance. The downside when I go out in the States is I've been accused of having a forged identification card."

Luisa stared out the window. "Looks like we'll be landing soon."

"In advance of that, I'd like to brief you on what to expect."

She turned toward me.

"A team will be joining us when we land at the Napa airfield. They will remain on your detail as long as necessary. It is unlikely you will be aware of their presence. However, you'll be meeting them upon our arrival." I handed her a cell phone. "I've programmed the necessary numbers into your new phone, including your sister's and mother's."

"What about Jada? She's my best friend."

"Ah, Yáñez, correct?" I'd forgotten to enter that particular number.

Luisa nodded.

"My apologies." I swiped the screen and entered her contact information.

"You know her number?" She seemed surprised.

"I'm afraid I've a photographic memory."

"That would've been useful when I was getting my MBA."

"There are times it's a curse as much as a blessing." It was actually far more often the former, but I didn't need to trouble Luisa with that detail.

We exited the aircraft and approached the SUVs waiting to transport us to Press' parents' estate in Napa.

"Luisa, I'd like to introduce Patton Abrams," I said.

"Most people call me Tank, ma'am," he said, shaking her hand.

"And this is Lavery Barrett, aka Press, and Vaile Oliver, who most call Zin," I continued, motioning Tank over to them.

"I'm Henry Bonham, code name Zeppelin, and this here is Magnet, uh, Justin…"

"Magnussen. I'm your best friend, and you don't know my bloody last name?" I chuckled when he slugged Zeppelin's arm. "Nice to meet you, miss," he said to Luisa.

"That's Atticus and Blackjack. You'll meet them later," said Magnet, pointing to the men currently surveilling our surroundings.

We got settled in the waiting vehicles. Press and Luisa rode with Zeppelin and Magnet while I was in the second SUV with Tank, Blackjack, Atticus, and Zin.

When we arrived at the gate, Press expressed concern that they were open via Magnet's comms.

We proceeded onto the property after Zeppelin suggested we get a vector. Once a few feet beyond the main entrance, Blackjack and Atticus got out of the vehicle, each going to the opposite sides of the residence. When we reached the front portico, I saw a woman standing outside the front door.

"That's Mrs. Gonzales, the Barretts' housekeeper," said Zin, exiting through the rear passenger door. I followed and listened as she informed him Mrs. Barrett had been transported via helicopter to a local hospital. Her husband had gone with her.

After receiving verification from the emergency services, confirming Gonzales' recounting, I instructed Tank to give Zep the all clear. We walked a fine line between ensuring her reports were accurate and we weren't putting our assets at risk, and withholding urgent information regarding Press' mother.

I stood back and watched, already knowing the news he would soon receive would be the worst he could imagine. In the next hour, his life would be shattered, but it wasn't my place to tell him. He needed to go to his father, needed to hear the devastating news directly from him.

When Magnet rushed Press back to the SUV and the two sped off, I led Luisa inside the house.

"Can I get you anything?" I asked.

"I could use a glass of wine."

"I'll get it," Zin offered. "Red or white?"

Luisa shrugged. "Either, please."

When he looked over at me, I shook my head and mouthed my thanks.

"I have a really bad feeling about this," I heard her say under her breath.

"Hmm, yes," I murmured when she glanced at me as if she expected me to respond.

"You know, don't you?"

I led her to the sofa and sat beside her. "Whenever someone is airlifted to a hospital, it means they are in critical condition. Otherwise, they would've transported Mrs. Barrett to a closer healthcare provider."

She nodded and looked toward the window. "Press is the best man I know. The best person, other than my sister. He's done so much for me."

I squeezed her hand. "He cares very much about you. It's evident."

She nodded. "And once again, he's looking out for me. I just wish I could be there for him, the way he always is for me."

"I could make a suggestion."

"I'd love to hear it."

"It's the little things that make a difference. Touching someone's hand, fetching them coffee, even a smile can mean everything. Especially when delivered by someone who matters." Images of Tryst raced through my head. His sweet gestures meant so much to me. I'd never forget our walks to the hilltop to watch the sunset. Particularly that first time, when he'd said he thought I could use a little magic.

"It sounds like you speak from experience."

"I suppose I do. There are certain people who care about others really well—love really well. I read an article about it. I have a strong feeling Press is one of them."

It was another two hours before we heard anything from him, and then, it was with the news I feared. Mrs. Barrett had passed.

I eavesdropped from outside the kitchen on Zin's side of the conversation and cringed when he asked Press if he should tell Luisa. No one had asked my opinion, but from what I'd witnessed thus far, Zin Oliver had all the sensitivity of a doorknob. That belief multiplied when I heard him suggest we'd discuss Luisa's relocation the following day.

His call ended and he was walking out of the kitchen when I intercepted him. "I'll tell her," I said emphatically enough it left no room for argument.

"Fine, but he doesn't want her here when he gets back."

I raised a brow. "He said that?"

"Not in so many words."

"Which words, Oliver?" I pressed.

"I suggested we relocate to one of the guesthouses, and he said he thought that would be for the best."

I had no doubt there was more to the conversation. However, if Press wanted to see Luisa upon his return, he would do so.

Her reaction was as I expected it to be. When she'd asked earlier, I had no doubt she'd sensed Press' mother was gone.

"We think it would be best if we went to the guesthouse to give him and his father privacy upon their return."

"Of course."

When Zin followed us, I sent Tank a text, asking that someone intercept the bastard. Given there was more than one guest accommodation, he could bloody well stay elsewhere.

A little over an hour after Press and his father returned, Luisa was standing by the window, looking at the main house, while I sat on the sofa, pretending to read a book.

"You can sleep if you want to," she'd said more than once.

"Not tired," I'd murmured in response.

When I saw her pick up her mobile and place a call, I stepped out of the room yet remained close enough to hear most of what was said.

"Press—" I raised my head and returned when I heard Luisa's voice crack.

"I have to go to him," she said, racing out the door. I knew Tank, Blackjack, and Atticus were close enough to cover us as I rushed out behind her. What I hadn't expected was to see Zin run past me, after her. What I would give for a stun gun.

"It's okay," I heard Press say to him when he reached the front door seconds after Luisa did.

I walked up behind them. "The house is secure," I said, motioning for Zin to step away. Instead, he grabbed my arm and closed the door behind us.

I immediately swung it down toward the meeting point between his thumb and finger—the weakest part of his hold—then yanked it free. At the same time, I put my hand on his wrist and jerked his arm behind his back. "Touch me again, and the consequences will be far worse," I seethed right before releasing him.

"What the fuck?" he bellowed.

"Lower your voice, sir. Your best friend has just suffered one of the greatest losses of his life. Show him the respect he deserves." I stalked off in the direction of the guesthouse.

"Let us know if you want backup," Tank said through the comms.

"Is he following?" I asked. I doubted he was, since I couldn't hear him. However, I didn't want to turn around and check.

"Negative."

"Then, no. However, it'll be in the man's best interest if he's encouraged to keep his distance."

I knew from the sound of his laugh it was Zeppelin I heard chuckling. "Maybe he needs a little fear of Unit 23 put in him."

"We'll allow him to live, given Press needs him. When the time comes he doesn't, we'll readdress."

I smiled when I heard their laughter through my earpiece. It had been a very long, equally trying day for everyone, but it was far worse for Press, his brother, and his father. I'd suffered the loss of someone far too young for their life to be over. While my own mum was still alive, as was my father, I knew their pain would not be any less than what I felt when my husband died. I took comfort in the fact that if anyone could help Press through this loss, it was Luisa.

At zero six hundred the following morning, I gathered the team together to review the goals of our mission.

"For all intents and purposes, our team is here to provide protection for Luisa Reeve. While that is true, our greater goal is to determine who is behind the auction site where she's up for bid. Additionally, to identify who wants her badly enough that they've offered a quarter of a million dollars."

"According to the brief, Poseidon and Oleander believe the AMPS organization is behind the auction," said Magnet.

"That is correct. The timing of it going live, as well as the increase in bids being registered, not just for Ms. Reeve but for the other women, indicates someone is administering the site. Which, in turn, rules out Mithras as our primary suspect."

"Zin mentioned relocation last night," said Tank. "By the way, Beau Barrett is scheduled to arrive before eleven hundred."

"Copy that. As far as the subject of relocation, I support the idea in that the Barretts will likely have family, friends, and neighbors wishing to pay their respects. The last thing we would want—Luisa would want—is to impede that process."

"Incoming," Atticus said through the comms. "Do you want me to intercept?"

I looked up and saw Zin stalking across the lawn in our direction. "Bloody hell. Negative on the intercept."

As was to be expected, Zin didn't hesitate to enter the guesthouse, nor did he apologize for interrupting what was clearly a meeting. "I've made arrangements for Luisa to stay with Laird and Sorcha Butler. She'll leave this morning."

Stunned to the point of near-speechlessness, I was grateful when Zeppelin stood. "We'll take this offline," he said, ushering Zin out of the guesthouse.

I raised a brow. "As Tank was saying, Luisa Reeve will be relocating…" Those remaining in the room chuckled. "As far as security is concerned, I'm sure everyone here is aware Laird, aka Burns, Butler is the mastermind behind the intelligence technology used by the US, the UK, and our trusted allies. There is no question Luisa will be equally safe there as she is here. More so, in fact." I turned to Magnet. "In Zep's absence, can you brief us on the latest developments in the hunt for Pharaoh?"

He stood and gave a rundown on the progress being made by the task forces whose joint command center was in the UK. While they'd had luck finding the first auction's IP origin, they hadn't yet with this one. He ended with, "Which means we have no idea where the women offered on the site are being held captive."

"Are we in agreement that whoever wants Luisa Reeve will stop at nothing to get her?" Atticus asked.

"Affirmative," I responded, looking directly at each person seated around the table. "And whoever it is will not lay a single finger on her under my watch."

9

Tryst

I'd just turned the page of the book I was reading when I heard a knock at my door.

"Hello, Brix," I said, embracing him when he stepped inside.

"There's no easy way to say this. Susannah Barrett passed away last night."

"No," I gasped, grabbing the back of the chair closest to me. "What happened?"

"According to Zin, a pulmonary embolism traveled to her heart."

I lowered my head. "Martin?"

"He's devastated, as you know from experience. The *caballeros* and *ancianos caballeros* are gathering in Napa."

"We're the *viejos*, nephew."

Brix half smiled and nodded. "I'm going to fly into San Luis Obispo tomorrow and drop Addison off with her mother before going to Napa for the services."

"I will join you."

During the flight, I thought about the *viejos caballeros*. When I joined, my brother, Alfonso, was the senior member, thus he led the meetings. He was the first of our generation we lost. Next was Brian Hope, who'd died six years ago, when he was thrown from a horse and suffered a skull fracture.

There were eight of us left—Hewitt Ridge, Michael Oliver, Martin Barrett, Baron Von Orr, George Norman, Malcolm Warwick, Charlie Jenson, and myself. Sadly, Martin was not the only widower besides me. Both Baron Von Orr and Malcolm Warwick had lost their wives in the years since my Rosa passed.

As for the *ancianos caballeros*, I remembered little of them, even of my own father, Cristobal. He was forty-three when I came along unexpectedly. Ten years later, he passed away.

"What?" Brix asked, perhaps noticing my scrunched eyes.

"My father was only one year older than yours was when he died."

"I guess I knew that, although I never really thought about it."

"I am fifty, so perhaps it is more relevant to me."

Brix shook his head. "You are in better physical condition than I am, Uncle."

"While you are taking Addy to her mother's, I need to stop by Los Caballeros."

"I'll go with you if you don't mind waiting."

"I don't want to delay our arrival in Napa. I will run my errand, then return to the airfield."

Brix nodded. "Understood."

I had no intention of sharing my reason for visiting Los Caballeros, since it would only be a quick stop after my real destination, where Jaicon and Luisa were. Quite simply, I wanted to see her. Perhaps it was more of a need.

I approached the gates of Butler Ranch and, once granted access, pulled up near the main residence, went to the front door, and knocked. Laird opened it, welcomed me inside, and we embraced like the two old friends we were.

"I'm here to speak with Jaicon before traveling to the Barrett estate," I said.

"Please give our condolences to Martin and to Press and Beau."

"I will."

He motioned to Jaicon, who stood not far from the kitchen.

"Tryst? I'm surprised to see you here," she said when I approached.

"I'm on my way to Napa and don't have much time. May I speak with you privately?"

"Of course."

I led her outside, to the front porch, longing to pull her into my arms and tell her how much I missed her, even after two days. I didn't, though. I merely rested my hand on the small of her back. "I am uncomfortable with the way we left things," I began. "The kiss—"

"Tryst, please do not apologize. We're both to blame."

"Blame?" My heart hurt. "While I regret how we parted, I do not regret kissing you."

When she turned away, I put my hand on her shoulder. "Please do not run from me again, Jacy."

She walked to the edge of the porch, hugged herself, and looked up at the sky. "A few minutes before it happened, I thought about the two of us and how *if only* we'd met in another time and another place, *if only* we weren't so far apart in age. It went on and on, Tryst."

I stepped closer, wishing she'd turn to me, but spoke anyway when she didn't. "If we'd met when Rosa or your husband were still alive, we would not have become more than acquaintances. I cannot dispute the age difference except to say it doesn't matter to me. If it does to you…" I shook my head.

"It doesn't, but there's more. You live in Mexico. I don't live anywhere. I can't remember the last time I spent more than a few days at my flat in London. And now, commanding this new unit, Merrigan said the base of operation could be anywhere. It would've been easier if she'd made the decision for me."

"She made no suggestions?"

"She did."

I breathed a sigh of relief when her eyes met mine. "Where, Jacy?"

"I asked if it would be necessary for me to work out of the UK or somewhere else in Eurasia, and she said it wasn't."

"Where?" I whispered.

"She said it could be in the US or even Mexico."

I smiled. "Alamos, Mexico?"

She rolled her eyes. "Where else, Tryst?"

"There are many advantages to you being there."

"Name one that has nothing to do with you and me and kissing."

"I have been working with you, have I not?"

"You could work with me in California."

"I could. However, there is another reason I think you should consider Mexico instead."

"What?"

"Cariño."

Her eyes filled with tears. "You don't play fair."

I nodded. "I play to win."

"What is winning, Tryst? What do you see happening between us?"

It was the hardest question she'd asked thus far. "I don't know, but I'd like to find out."

"I don't know either, and it frightens me."

When she went inside, I didn't follow.

Brix and I didn't speak much on the plane ride from San Luis Obispo to Napa, nor did we on the hour drive from the airfield to the Barrett estate.

Over the course of the next three days, the *caballeros*—both the youngsters, as I'd begun referring to them, and the *viejos*—did our best to support Martin, Press, and Beau Barrett, helping them navigate the loss of their wife and mother.

Susannah Barrett was buried on the morning of the third day, and that afternoon, I offered to stay on longer if Martin wanted me to. When he insisted it wasn't necessary, I caught a flight to San Luis Obispo, unsure where I should go from there. I was about to book a commercial flight to Alamos when I received a call from Sorcha Butler.

"Martin and Press are on their way here now," she said. "Press misses Luisa, and she misses him. As for Martin, I don't think he's quite ready to be on his own yet. Will you join us?"

Rather than respectfully decline, I shamefully took advantage of the opportunity to see Jaicon once more before returning to my ranch. "I will, and thank you for the invitation, my friend."

"You are always welcome here, Tryst. This, you know. Besides, I think there is another person here who will be as happy to see you as I will." I didn't need to close my eyes to picture her winking with her words.

Driving through the gates reminded me of being here only a few days ago and of the way Jaicon and I left things—again. I hadn't thought much about it while I was in Napa. My focus had been on a man who was like a brother to me and his sons. Now, though, the separation I felt between us came roaring back at me like the onset of a powerful and deadly storm. If I hadn't told Sorcha I'd come, I'd turn around, return to the airfield, and catch the next flight home.

Instead, I parked the car and made the trek up the porch steps. When I walked into the house, the first person I saw, even though she was on the opposite side of the room, was Jaicon. I greeted the others as I hurried past them in her direction.

"Hello," I said, stopping abruptly but not until we were almost toe-to-toe.

Her smile warmed my chilled heart. "Hello, Tryst."

My arms dangled at my sides, fists clenched, wishing I could cup her cheek with my palm instead, kiss her, tell her how painful every minute away from her had been.

We chatted amiably for what seemed like mere minutes but in actuality was closer to a couple of hours. I filled her in on Cariño's progress and shared a video I received from Tex. We talked about how Sorcha made it her mission to get everyone to eat five times the amount they'd normally consume.

All too soon, Martin and his son announced they were leaving for Seahorse, Press' oceanfront estate in the coastal community of Cambria.

"I suppose I should leave as well," I said when I realized they'd been gone for close to a half hour.

Jaicon's eyes bored into mine. "What's your plan?"

"I'm not sure I understand the question."

"Do you intend to continue consulting with K19 Allied Intelligence?"

"As long as I'm needed."

She smiled. "You're needed, Tryst."

Jaicon walked me to the door, and just as I was about to say good night, we heard a scream from one of the second-story bedrooms. She raced up the stairs with me, along with several others, behind her.

Seraphina and Jada rushed over to Luisa at the same time I spotted a cell phone on the floor in the corner of the room. I picked it up and gave it to Jacy.

"What is it?" I asked.

She handed the phone back to me. On the screen was a grainy image of a naked woman. Her arms and legs were bound and spread, tied to four hooks protruding from the wall she faced. Crisscrossing marks on her back appeared to be bleeding. The only other thing visible in the photo was a man's hand holding a whip.

The accompanying message read, "Your punishment awaits, my Luisa. Next time, you won't escape before we've had our fun."

"I'm going to ask Press to return," Jaicon whispered. "Can you update the team while I do?"

"Of course." I followed her out of the room and downstairs. While she placed the call, I briefed the five K19 operatives, Laird, and Sorcha on what had transpired.

"My God," Sorcha gasped.

"He's on his way," Jacy said, approaching us. "Let's take this outside." As we made our way to the front porch, I saw her hand Laird the phone. "Please see if you can trace where the message came from." Zeppelin followed him in the opposite direction we were headed.

I wasn't surprised she'd asked. He would be able to get the information she requested faster than anyone else.

"We won't know much until we can trace the call," she began. "However, my prediction is Luisa will not want to remain here, regardless of whether this is the safest place for her."

I agreed with both statements. I doubted the White House had security in place on par with Butler Ranch.

"I'd prefer to wait until Press arrives to discuss other options. Luisa is most comfortable with him, even over her mother and sister."

Within minutes, Zeppelin joined us with an update. "The message originated from the Middle East. Specifically, Egypt. The device used to contact Luisa was immediately destroyed. However, we're reaching out for help from our friends at the NRO."

Less than an hour later, Jaicon was proven correct in assuming Luisa did not want to stay here. After several options were discussed, including my own ranch, she and Press chose to return to Napa.

One of Laird and Sorcha's sons, Naughton, who lived on the estate with his wife and son, was a helicopter pilot and kept one on the property. He offered to transport them immediately.

"I will remain here until you request otherwise," I told Jacy when she was preparing to board the helicopter along with Zeppelin, Press, and Luisa. Tank, Magnet, Blackjack, and Atticus were traveling via SUV with Martin.

"I appreciate it," she said, stunning me when she stepped forward and embraced me.

When I returned to the house, I found Laird seated on the front porch, smoking his pipe. "May I join you?" I asked.

"By all means." He motioned to one of the chairs.

We sat in silence for several minutes. I was sure, like me, he was thinking about the events of the last few days.

"You and I have been friends for many years," he began. "However, you are closer in age to my eldest son than to me, so please forgive me if I offer some fatherly advice."

"Your advice will always be welcome in whatever manner it is given."

"It will not come as any surprise to you to hear I have intervened with my wife about her penchant for matchmaking."

I chuckled. "I appreciate it. My niece—your daughter-in-law—does her best to fill in whatever gaps Sorcha leaves."

He laughed, pulled a tobacco pouch from his pocket, and refilled the bowl of his pipe. "I fear you will soon lump me in with the two of them."

"No, Laird! Say it isn't so."

This time, we both laughed.

"It has been years since I've seen you look so happy, Tryst, and there is no question as to the person responsible for your renewed spirit. Jaicon is a lovely, intelligent person. As long as Sorcha doesn't get wind of it, I will add she is extraordinarily beautiful."

"I agree with everything you've said."

Laird leaned forward. "It's okay to love again, Tryst. You know in your heart it's what Rosa would want for you."

"You are right."

"I am so happy to hear you agree."

I shook my head. "However, it isn't up to me, Laird. I made my feelings known. Now, the ball is in Jaicon's court, as they say." It struck me that tomorrow was New Year's Eve. Like every other year, I had no plans. Today, I wished so much I did.

"Come on, old man," Laird said to me. "You can stay in Angus House."

I raised a brow. "You've named the cottages, eh?"

"Sorcha and I have grown weary of saying, 'Maddox's old place' or 'Naught's.'"

"I would've thought you'd go with Burns' Place or Rua's Run."

"Now, there's an idea!" he said, lighting his pipe on the way to the cottage.

10

Jaicon

"Esencia, long time," said Oleander when I placed the video call to her the following day.

"How are you, O?"

"While currently flying to Egypt on a quest to find Pharaoh, I feel a bit like my wings have been clipped."

I chuckled. Even if I hadn't accepted the appointment to Unit 23, I was well aware one of the benefits of being part of the elite team was the absence of many of the rules those of us with more visible assignments had to deal with.

"This feels like a major screwup on the part of whoever sent the message to Ms. Reeve," I suggested.

"I wholeheartedly agree, particularly given the NRO has already triangulated the location. We're headed to it as we speak."

"Excellent news. Godspeed, O."

"Once this mission is complete, we need to chat, my friend."

I cut the feed without responding. Oleander had lobbied hard for me to join the unit. However, with the challenges I faced with my memory, joining a team whose missions often involved assassination wasn't wise.

I went into the other room, where Zeppelin, Magnet, and Tank were waiting.

"Any news on the Pharaoh search?" Zep asked. Pharaoh, who both O and Zeppelin had referenced, was believed to be a key player in one of the largest human trafficking rings, one that was hosting a sex-slave auction on the dark web.

"O is on her way to the triangulation area now."

"I hope to fucking hell they find Pharaoh," muttered Zep.

"I do too."

"Has there been an update as to when the bidding is scheduled to go live?" Tank asked.

"Affirmative. It's been delayed," I responded.

"Which means the organizers are holding out hope they can get their hands on Luisa Reeve before then."

I'd had the same thought.

"Looks like they're in for the night," reported Blackjack when he and Atticus returned close to dinner time. Tank and Magnet were responsible for the next eight-hour shift, patrolling the grounds.

"Happy New Year's Eve, everyone," Tank said, waving as he walked out the door.

I couldn't say I'd forgotten the holiday; I just hadn't thought about it. What I did think about—or who—was Tryst. He lingered in the back of my mind constantly to the point where I found myself inventing reasons I needed him to come to Napa. None sounded plausible enough for me to request his presence. However, I still wished he was here.

My husband hadn't been one to celebrate holidays. Like me, he spent so many on a mission in some corner of the world where it was difficult to decipher one day from the next.

"If you don't mind, I think I'll take a walk," I said to Zeppelin, who was monitoring the three computer screens where the security feeds appeared in real time.

"Take all the time you need."

I didn't know Zeppelin well enough to ask him whether he typically celebrated the new year, in the same way none of us brought up working on Christmas. In our business, the mission always came first.

As I walked across the lawn of the Barrett estate, I looked up at the cloudless sky. The air was clear in Napa, and tonight, the stars were on brilliant display. Tryst and I had spent many nights staring at the constellations in the same way I was now. While I could remember every moment visually, I had a tough time recalling what we'd talked about. All I knew for certain was I'd never been bored. Not for a single minute I spent with the man.

I carried my mobile in my hand but was still startled when it vibrated. I smiled when I looked at the screen and saw it was Tryst calling.

"Were your ears burning?"

He chuckled. "I could ask you the same thing. How goes it in Napa?"

"Seemingly calm presently. Press and Luisa are enjoying a quiet evening. They both need it so badly."

"I agree. What about you?" he asked.

"I'm out walking, looking up at the night sky, remembering all the times we spent doing the same thing at your ranch."

"I miss you."

His blunt statement left me breathless. "I miss you, Tryst."

"I've been trying to think of a reason to join you in Napa."

I laughed. "Me too."

"Ah. It warms my heart to hear you say so."

"Where are you?"

"In Angus House."

"Come again?"

"It is one of the cottages on Butler Ranch. Laird told me tonight that he and Sorcha have decided to give them names."

"How very Scottish of them."

He sighed. "What I would give to see your smile."

"It would be quite easy. We could have a video chat instead of a phone call."

"Yes, that's right. I am not as technologically advanced as you youngsters are."

"You say that as a guest on the estate owned by one of the most technologically advanced men on the planet, who is also at least twenty years older than you are.”

“Laird would be disappointed in me.”

“Hang up, and I’ll ring you back.”

“I hope I can figure out how to answer.”

“Now, you’re just being obtuse.” I ended the call and did as I said I would. Tryst picked up immediately. I sighed as I gazed at the face of the man I so wished was here with me.

“Jaicon by moonlight, one of my very favorite things in life.”

“You are a very handsome man, Tryst.”

He raked his beard with his hand. “Gray and all?”

“Especially gray. I believe I’ve told you before it suits you.”

His eyes twinkled even as they scrunched with his smile. “You are good for my ego, Jacy. More than my ego; you are good for me.”

I sat down on the grass. “I’m sorry I said not knowing what would happen between us frightens me.”

Tryst shook his head. “Do not apologize for being honest.”

“You said you’d like to find out.”

"I was being honest as well."

"I would too."

He closed his eyes. "There are no words I wished to hear more this New Year's Eve."

"None?"

He shook his head and laughed. "I will admit to fantasizing about others. However, just knowing you are open to seeing where this journey takes us fills me with joy."

"Tell me your fantasy." I could feel the heat of his gaze through the phone.

"I will, but first, I need you to return inside. You look chilled."

"I'm missing the *chimenea* too."

"Tell me when you are alone as I am, and I will begin."

"Do you want me to ring you back?"

"No. I will stay with you as you walk."

He remained silent until after I was inside the guest-house and had shut the bedroom door.

"I'm alone, Tryst."

"Put the phone down but keep it somewhere close."

I set it in the charging cradle on the bedside table.

"Lie down, and I will do the same."

I stretched out on my side and looked up at the mobile's screen.

"The first night I had this fantasy, we were in Montecito, staying with Kade and Merrigan. You were in the bedroom next to me."

My cheeks flushed. I'd fantasized about him then too.

"It is only fair you share your thoughts with me, Jaicon."

I smiled. "I thought about you too."

"Ah, that will be for another night. Now, lie on your back and close your eyes."

There was just enough of an edge to his voice that I shuddered.

"You hear the door open and the sound of my footsteps as I approach the bed. When I slide in beside you, I hold your naked body against me."

"God, Tryst."

"Are you naked, Jacy?"

"No."

"I will wait."

I ripped at my clothes, pulling them from my body. "Okay. I am."

"I take your lips, kissing you like I've longed to since the first moment we met. You're needy, demanding I remove my boxers so I'm naked like you are. You wrap your soft hand around my hardness and spread your legs. Do it now, Jacy. Spread your legs for me."

I whimpered and did as he told me.

"I want your hands and mouth on me, but I cannot allow it now."

"Why not?"

"Because I must taste you. I need your essence on my tongue. Will you let me?"

"Yes."

"Touch your pussy. Are you wet for me?"

"So wet."

"Run your fingers through your folds and show me."

I did and held my fingers close to the mobile's screen. Tryst groaned.

"Those are *my* fingers, Jaicon. I swirl your clit with them and thrust them inside you. You come."

I cried out as pleasure spread throughout my body.

"I have to be inside you. I cannot wait a moment more. I remove my fingers and spread your legs. Your back arches as my cock enters your heat. You beg me to go deeper, harder, faster. Can you feel me?"

"Yes," I cry, on the verge of another orgasm.

"Come now, Jacy. Let me hear my name on your lips as yours is on mine."

I shattered in ecstasy. I had no words. Nothing but his name. *Tryst.*

"Jaicon?" I could hear him, but his voice was floating somewhere in the ether. "Come back to me, beautiful girl."

I rolled to my side, opened my eyes, and nearly gasped when I saw his beautiful face.

"They say whatever you're doing when the clock strikes midnight on the first day of the new year is how your year will continue."

"Midnight?"

"Happy New Year, my love." He ended the call.

I was sitting by the window, staring at nothing, remembering every second of my video call with Tryst, wishing over and over again he was here in Napa with me.

"Hey, Esencia," said Tank, who was on security-monitor duty.

I stood and walked over to him. "Yes?"

"We just intercepted a message that came to Luisa's new phone."

"Bloody hell," I muttered. "Who is this fucker, and how is he getting access to phones that are locked up tighter than the UK Prime Minister's?" Perhaps that was a bad example, given things were repeatedly leaked from that particular source. "What is it?"

Tank hit play on the video. In it, a woman was tied to a wall in the same way the woman in the photo sent with the previous message had been.

"Luisa, my Luisa," the voice began. "I told you. Next time, you won't escape before we've had our fun. Sadly, your best friend beat you to it." The voice cackled. "She begged so prettily for me to let her go that I finally agreed to her suggestion. When she said, 'Trade me for her,' I had to admit it was a brilliant solution." There were more cackles. "Here is how it will go. When you arrive, I will be standing with the barrel of my gun resting against your best friend's temple. If I hear any voice or see any face other than yours, she will die instantly. Reply to this message with the words 'I'm yours' to receive your next set of instructions." The screen went black.

"He's got Jada Yáñez."

In the time it took for me to watch the video a second time, Tank confirmed with Atticus that Luisa was secure and with Press and didn't seem to have received the message directly, which meant the interception tools we'd employed worked.

"Zeppelin sent me back in his place," said Magnet, who had run from the main house. "I was on my way here anyway," he added. "No less than ten minutes ago, Luisa mentioned to Press that she's been trying to reach Jada."

"I'm working on a trace," Tank reported just as Blackjack arrived, also from the direction of the main house.

"We need to act on this immediately," I said, pointing to Tank and Magnet. "You two come with me."

"Jada Yáñez is missing," Press blurted when he opened the door and we walked into the main house.

"We intercepted something," I said, looking between him and Luisa.

"What?" he asked.

"Another message."

Luisa gripped Press' arm.

"Give us a minute," he said, leading her out of the room.

When they didn't return after five, I went looking for them. "Press? This is urgent," I said when I found them.

"You're certain you want to do this?" I heard him ask Luisa.

"I can as long as you're with me."

"Come in," he said, motioning to me.

"It was sent from Ms. Yáñez's phone," I began.

"Is she alive?" Luisa whispered.

"She is."

"He has her, doesn't he?"

I nodded.

"My God," Press said under his breath at the same time Luisa looked up at me.

"Tell me," she said, squaring her shoulders.

I sat beside her. "What you're about to see is a video of a woman we believe is Ms. Yáñez. She has been tortured. The person who sent it has very specific instructions. He will free Ms. Yáñez—"

"Her name is Jada."

I nodded. "My apologies. He said he will free Jada in exchange for Luisa."

Press shook his head. "No fucking way."

"What are the instructions?" Luisa asked.

Press continued to shake his head.

"What are they?" she shouted.

"He wants you to come to where he's holding her. He said if he sees or hears anyone other than you, he'll kill her."

"Where?"

"Once he receives a response to his message, he'll tell you where to go."

"This is ludicrous," Press muttered.

Luisa looked at me. "I want to see it."

When he refused to relent, I stood and walked over to the window. It wasn't up to me. However, if Luisa wanted to see it, Press should not stop her from doing so. I turned to face them when I heard her say my name.

Press nodded, and I called out to Magnet to join us.

He placed a tablet on the table and spoke directly to Luisa. "The voice has been digitally enhanced to make it unrecognizable, and the only person visible is Jada."

"Go ahead," she told him.

When the video concluded, I picked up the tablet. "Zeppelin is working to triangulate the location using cell towers. Once we've done that, we'll use overheads to get a clear read on where Jada is being held."

Luisa shook her head. "Don't bother. I know where she is."

"Where?" asked Press.

"I'll show you," she said, pointing to the tablet.

I returned it to Magnet, and as soon as the video began, Luisa pointed to the upper right corner.

"See that? It's an on-air sign."

"Like for a radio or TV show?" Tank asked.

"Yes." She pointed at it again. "Look at the lower left corner. Part of it is cracked, and someone tried to fix it with blue adhesive. It's at the SLO underground radio station. Jada and I did an internship there when we were in high school."

I looked over at Zeppelin. "Transport is on the way."

I stepped closer to Tank. "Keep the NRO on this. We need every detail, every schematic of the building where this is located. Everything possible they can get to us."

I cringed inwardly when I heard Press say Zin Oliver had also worked there. I was aware of the clandestine relationship between him and Jada, and the last thing any of us needed was his interference.

"Get in touch with Doc," I said to Zep at the same time I stepped out of the room to ring Tryst.

"Laird has just informed us Jada is being held captive," he said in a low voice when he answered my call.

"Tell me, is Zin there?"

Before he could answer, I heard the man's voice bellowing in the background. *"Where the fuck does this sonuvabitch have her?"*

"You'll receive updates as we know more," I heard Press say from the other room.

I looked out the window and saw an Akicita transport helicopter descending on the lawn. "We're mobilizing," I said to Tryst.

"Doc and the rest of the K19 operatives here at Butler Ranch are about to do the same thing. Should I go with them?"

"Affirmative. And Tryst, do not allow Zin Oliver to follow."

"Roger that. Wait, he was just here." Tryst put his hand over the receiver for a few seconds. "Jacy?"

"I'm still here."

"He's gone."

"Bloody fucking hell. See if you can find him."

"I will."

"The NRO just confirmed the location," said Tank when I rang off.

"Copy that. Let's move out," I ordered, rushing over to the French doors that led outside.

"Wait!" I heard Luisa shout from behind me. "I'm going too."

My eyes met Press', and I nodded. If we couldn't get the schematics in time, she may be the only one who could help us find the station's location expediently. I stepped aside for the two to board.

"Los Caballeros," Press mouthed as he climbed in and took his seat.

While I nodded in response, I prayed one *caballero* would stay out of the way and not get himself or Jada killed.

11

Tryst

"That stupid fucking *sonuvabitch*," I heard Onyx seethe as he followed behind Doc, who rushed into the main residence at Butler Ranch with Jada in his arms.

He carried her into the back hallway, where a triage room had been set up two years ago when a fire raged out of control on the vineyard property and several ranch workers were injured.

Dalton "Bones" Ridge, a current member of Los Caballeros and a doctor, had shown up a few minutes ago to prepare for Jada's arrival.

Seconds later, Jaicon walked through the door. I'd seen her from a distance at the raid on the radio station, but I wasn't able to speak to her. I walked in her direction and met her halfway.

"Tryst, I—"

"Come with me," I said when I saw her eyes fill with tears. I put my hand on the small of her back and led her outside. Rather than stopping on the front porch, I kept going to Angus House, where I'd spent the last two nights. Once inside, I didn't hesitate. I pulled her into my arms and held her as she cried.

After a few minutes, I felt her shudders subsiding, but I had no intention of letting go.

"Tryst, you must think I'm—"

I cut her off again but, this time, with my mouth. Her soft lips tasted salty from her tears, and I lost myself in them, tentatively pressing them open with my tongue. I cupped her nape with my palm and deepened the kiss.

When her tongue moved against mine, I was suddenly ravenous, demanding more of what she so willingly gave.

"Jaicon," I said, nipping her bottom lip. Rather than back away, she weaved her fingers into my hair, pulling until our mouths were fused once again.

I snaked my arm around her waist, needing her closer. When she wrapped one leg around me and ground herself against my thigh, I withdrew from her mouth and trailed kisses down the side of her neck to the hollow of her throat.

"Wait," she said, separating her body from mine like I had our lips. "I can't. I mean, I want to, but Jada, and…"

I rested my forehead against hers but kept my arms around her. "Do not explain. We gave each other momentary comfort after facing the worst kind of evil. That is all."

"Can we sit for a minute?" she asked.

"Of course." I took her hand and led her to the sofa, where we sat in silence for several minutes. "Do you want to talk about what happened?"

"*Zin,*" she spat. "I was within seconds of issuing the order to move in when shots were fired."

"I was there. However, I wasn't briefed on exactly what was happening."

"We received the building's schematic from the NRO while en route in the Akicita. Luisa was able to confirm which corridors had access to the area where Jada was being held. That place was built like a bloody rat maze. Anyway, shortly after we completed mapping our plan of attack, Atticus compiled a list of everyone who worked at the station since its inception. It took Luisa less than ten seconds to identify a man who had harassed her when they shared classes in the MBA program—Hamad Al Zaabi."

"He is the man Zin shot."

Jaicon nodded. "That's right. Atticus pulled a dossier while Magnet contacted the NRO. Within minutes, he reported reconnaissance was able to place him in Egypt four days ago, when the first message was sent." She took a deep breath. "He had every bloody corridor mapped, like we had, meaning he'd be able to see and hear from wherever we entered. His threat was that unless Luisa came in alone, he would kill Jada."

"I was with Burns when he intercepted the signals and replaced the feeds."

"As we made our descent, I made contact with Al Zaabi using Luisa's mobile, which generated an auto-response reminding her what would happen if she did not arrive alone and that the clock was ticking. She had exactly thirty minutes."

I told her I was on the scene when the helicopter touched down and the teams moved into position.

"So you're aware we had everything in place. Ten sniper-trained operatives would've had him surrounded. Any one of us could've neutralized Al Zaabi before he had the chance to pull the trigger on the gun he had trained on Jada. Instead, out of nowhere, Zin fucking shoots to kill." Her cell rang, and she swiped the screen. "Hey, Fatale. I'll be right up." She ended the call and stood. "I'm sorry, but they need me at the main residence."

"We'll go together. I want to check on Jada."

When we reached the porch steps, Jaicon remained with Kade and Merrigan, who had been waiting for her, while I went inside. When I heard shouting coming from the direction of the triage room, I hurried down the hallway and opened the door when I recognized both Jada's brother Montano's voice and Zin's.

"I'll take it from here," I said, stepping into the room.

Montano looked over his shoulder. "It's okay, Tryst. I've got this."

"I was not asking for your permission, Montano."

"If I go, he goes." He pointed at Zin.

I took a step forward. "You'll both go."

Once I was sure they were doing as I'd asked, I approached Jada's bed, leaned down, and kissed her cheek.

"Hi, Tryst," she said, wincing.

"How bad is the pain?" I asked.

"Maybe a seven."

"I am sorry this happened to you, Jada."

She closed her eyes and whispered her thanks.

"What can I do to help?"

"I honestly don't know."

"Are you able to rest?"

She shook her head.

"Will you hold my hands?" I put them on her lap, and she rested her palms in mine. "Make yourself comfortable but keep your eyes focused on me. I will tell you a story."

"Okay," she whispered.

"I was on a walk in Mexico one day. I was young, younger than you are now, and I got lost. Since I was in the Army at the time, I couldn't admit to anyone that a survivalist got himself lost in the wilderness, so I kept going, hoping I would come to a trail or, better, a road."

"Or another person?"

I smiled. "While you may think you know the story, I'm going to share a few things I've never told anyone."

While Jada drifted in and out of sleep, I told her about the day I'd stumbled on the property that was now my ranch. It was the same day I met my Rosa, who had been traveling with her family at the time.

I told her about the creek she and I had found while we walked together that day, talking as though we were old friends who'd known each other for years rather than strangers who had just met.

"We crested a hillside and gasped as our eyes took in the view of the entire El Palomar valley. I told my Rosa I'd build her a house on the very ground we stood. It was a promise I kept," I said, watching as Jada fell into a deep sleep. Minutes later, she woke with a start. Her eyes were wide when she looked up at me.

"What did you see?" I asked when she tightened her hold on my hands.

"A coyote. It was approaching me."

I nodded. While Jada wasn't ready to hear it, I was convinced she'd just met her spirit animal. The one who would help her find her way to healing.

It wasn't long before Jada fell back to sleep. I waited about thirty minutes, then went to Angus House to rest as well.

I was about to switch on the light in the bedroom when I saw Jaicon. She must've dozed off while waiting for me, since she was fully dressed, lying on top of the bedclothes. I toed off my shoes, grabbed two throws, and covered her with one.

When I returned from using the bathroom, she still hadn't woken, so I lay next to her and used the second throw for myself. As exhausted as I was, it was less than a minute or two before I was asleep too.

When I opened my eyes the next morning, Jaicon and I had both shifted in our sleep. Her back was to my front, and I had my arm draped over her. It had been so long since I'd slept with another's body next to mine; I'd forgotten the comfort it provided. Her warmth soothed me to the point I almost drifted off again. However, I didn't want her to wake and feel uncomfortable. Before I could ease my body from hers, she opened her eyes and looked over her shoulder.

"Good morning," I said.

"Um. Hi."

I smiled when I tried to move my arm and she held onto it.

"You're warm."

"So are you."

"What time did you…you know?"

"Come to bed?"

She chuckled. "In a manner of speaking."

"After midnight."

"I can't believe I didn't wake up." Jaicon covered her mouth when she yawned. "I don't want to get out of bed."

I snuggled closer. "Me neither."

"What time is it?"

"Seven. Far too early to be awake."

She laughed. "Tell me you usually sleep later."

I wanted to tell her that if I woke up with her in my arms every morning, I might be awake, but I would certainly spend the rest of the day in bed if she'd join me. I shifted when I felt my cock hardening at the thought.

"I have a meeting with the team at zero eight hundred. Whoever the arsehole was who scheduled it so early is in big trouble."

"I'm guessing you scheduled it."

She smiled over her shoulder. "And as much as I'd like to stay right where I am and forget yesterday's events, I cannot."

"I should check on Jada," I said when she sat up.

"How was she last night?"

"Frail, but there were signs of the girl I've known since she was a toddler."

"Her recovery won't be easy."

I murmured my agreement.

Jaicon was looking at something on her phone, and her brow furrowed.

"Anything I can help with?"

"Tank was looking for me. He has my bag. I suppose it wouldn't do to tell him to bring it here."

I walked over to her. "I will make arrangements to get it from him and bring it here myself."

"I suppose, that way, you don't have to explain."

My brow furrowed like hers had been. "I have no reason to keep your staying here a secret. Unless, of course, you want me to."

"I just assumed…Well, you know what they say about that."

"I wouldn't want anyone to know?"

She nodded. "Then again, it isn't as if anything happened."

"I consider the kiss we shared to be something. Waking up with you in my arms, that was too."

"Tryst…"

"Whatever it is, say it. I will respect your wishes."

"I want to spend time with you, meaning when we're not working. I just…it doesn't feel right. I mean, intimacy."

"I agree."

We embraced, and she put her head on my chest. "I really like you, Tryst."

I smiled. "I really like you too."

She leaned up, brushed my lips with hers, then let go. "I should probably change into clothes I haven't slept in."

"Take a shower. I'll retrieve your bag. It will be waiting for you here when you're finished. If you need anything else, I won't be far. I'm going to check on Jada."

"Such a gentleman."

I grinned and winked. "Not always."

12

Jaicon

As I walked to the winery where our team meeting would take place, I remembered something I'd said at a previous briefing. I'd been referring to whoever had sent the first message to Luisa and vowed that he would not lay a finger on her under my watch. Instead, he'd gotten Jada.

"Hello, mind if I join you?" Merrigan asked, walking up beside me.

"Not at all. I should've thought to ask."

She shook her head. "This is your team. You are its commander, and I've no intention of usurping your position of authority. Nor would I with Onyx and the Shadow Ops."

"I appreciate it."

"I'm going to shift into the role of your friend now."

I raised a brow. "It makes me anxious when you preface whatever you're about to say in such a way."

She smiled. "Tryst."

"Yes. Tryst. Well, whatever your question may be, I likely do not have an answer."

"You care about him."

"Not a question, but yes. I do."

"And vice versa."

"We're, how shall I say this? Taking baby steps. Also, the timing of whatever it is, is horrible."

She nodded. "You know my opinion of him."

"If I remember correctly, he's a god among men."

"And you, Jacy, are a goddess."

"Incoming," I said, looking behind her.

"We'll pick this up later."

I shook my head. "We will not."

After we entered the winery, Merrigan smiled and took a seat on the room's perimeter.

The space filled with the men who'd been on Luisa's duty in Napa, along with Doc and Tryst, who I was surprised to see. I said so when he approached.

"Jada is resting, and Kade suggested I join you. If you'd rather I didn't—"

"I'm glad you're here."

When he smiled and took a seat, I walked over to Merrigan. "I invited Onyx, given he was part of the op yesterday, but he hasn't responded. I sent the text last night."

"I expected him as well. I'll check with Kade."

I returned to the front of the room. "We're waiting on one more. Let's give it another five minutes."

My eyes met Merrigan's, and she shook her head. I understood it to mean Onyx would not be attending.

"I take that back. Let's get started."

We reviewed the op step-by-step until we reached the part where Zin shot Al Zaabi.

"What do we know about how he was able to enter the building undetected?" I asked.

"I can answer that," said Doc. "He was privy to our replacement of Al Zaabi's feeds."

It now made sense that Onyx wasn't in attendance, and if he didn't yet know what Doc had just told the rest of us, I was glad he didn't hear it here first.

Tank pushed his chair back, rested his elbows on his knees, and hung his head. I gave him a minute, and when he looked up at me, I nodded.

"I may be in the minority here"—he looked around the room—"but that asshole has to suffer some reper-cussions. He used information you showed him the *courtesy* of sharing with him to interfere in an op, where we came damned close to losing an asset. What we did lose was the opportunity to interrogate Al Zaabi. The cost of which we may never know. How many lives might have been saved?" He shook his head and looked down at the floor a second time.

"You're not in the minority, mate," said Zeppelin. "In fact, I'd wager everyone in this room agrees with you."

"You can add my name to the list of those who do. However, I cannot speak about repercussions presently." I looked over at Merrigan, who nodded.

"Anyone else?"

"I haven't received a briefing from Shere today. Have you?"

Zeppelin referred to the city where the command center of the joint task forces of the UN Coalition Against Human Trafficking was located. Zep was the commander of the Swiss unit, and Magnet was the commander of the Albanian team.

"The last report I received said they were not successful in Egypt," I responded.

He nodded. "I'll follow up at our conclusion."

"Copy that." I looked around the room. "Anything else before we move on?"

When no one responded, I split the team into three groups. The first—Tank, Blackjack, and Atticus—would remain on Luisa Reeve's detail, most likely in Napa. The second—Tryst and I—would transition to Jada Yáñez's detail in the event whoever was working with Al Zaabi had also targeted her. Unless something transpired in the interim or Ares needed the three men he suggested to provide support for another op, the third group—Zeppelin and Magnet—would return to Shere.

"Once we know exactly what Ms. Reeve's and Ms. Yáñez's plans are, we'll work out relocations."

When I adjourned the meeting, Doc, Merrigan, and Tryst remained behind.

"I want you to know I'm closely monitoring the situation with Onyx. He's a live wire, which is completely understandable. However, he's made some threats we need to neutralize," said Doc.

"Tryst, what would you think about Jada going to your ranch for a time?" Merrigan asked.

He ran his hand over his beard. "There is a reason I named it the Healing Place. I would certainly be in favor of it as long as Jada is comfortable."

"Onyx did suggest she stay with Blanca and him in Canada Lake," said Doc. "Like Tryst said, the decision is hers, but I don't see that as the ideal, especially at this time of the year."

Tryst's brow was furrowed.

"What are you thinking?" I asked.

"The two have never been close. With the anger I feel coming off him, I would not recommend such a move."

"Another option is she goes to her mother's. She's been living there while she attended school," Doc added.

"What about Zin?" I asked.

"Please elaborate," said Merrigan.

"They have been in a relationship, albeit a secret one, for quite some time. It's clearly out in the open now. Do you think she'd want to stay with him?"

Merrigan nodded. "That would be another option. Of the four, my personal opinion is *El Lugar de Curación* is the best place for her, but as Tryst said, it will be Jada's decision."

"If there is nothing else, Merrigan and I need some mom-dad-and-kiddo time."

Tryst smiled. "I envy you. Enjoy." He turned to me. "Would you like to join me on a walk? It is a beautiful day for it."

We wandered beyond the vineyards and up a hillside. At its crest, there was a one-hundred-and-eighty-degree view of the Pacific Ocean. "I bet the sunset is spectacular here," I commented when he led me to a bench.

"You would win the wager."

I studied him. "You're quiet, Tryst. What's on your mind?"

He reached his arm behind me and pulled me close to him. "I am troubled about Montano—Onyx. While my brother's wife is his mother's twin—so he is not actually related to me—when they were growing up, he and his siblings called me their uncle."

"As Doc said, it's understandable he'd be upset over what happened to his sister."

"It is the threat he's alluded to that troubles me. He intends to take down Los Caballeros."

I was somewhat surprised Tryst was so forthright. However, he knew I was aware of the secret society. "What would that entail?"

"Exposing…certain things."

"I see."

"One of the previous members—Zin's father, in fact—has called an emergency meeting. It will take place tonight, and we will address the threat."

"How worried are you?"

"More about him than his intention. Los Caballeros has weathered many storms throughout the years. The *viejos*, which is my generation, had our fair share."

I smiled. "You're hardly old, Tryst."

"I appreciate you saying so. My nephew referred to us as the *ancianos* recently. I told him they were my father's generation."

We both took in the breathtaking view for several minutes.

"What is on *your* mind, Jaicon?"

"I've been thinking about your comment to Doc about envying his time with his children."

"You're wondering why I never had any of my own."

"If it's none of my business—"

He tightened his hold on me. "If there is something I don't wish to discuss, I will say so. I expect you to do the same."

"Fair enough."

"Rosa and I tried for many years. It was a visit to the doctor to look into fertility treatments that led to the cancer diagnosis."

I rested my head on his shoulder. "I'm so sorry."

"After that, we never discussed the matter of not being able to have children again. Which means we never learned the reason we couldn't."

"I understand."

"What about you and your husband? Did you discuss having a family?"

"We did not." It was a lie, both in fact and by omission, but I wasn't ready to talk about it. I might never be.

Our return walk was quiet, and rather than be comfortable in the silence, I felt as though a wall—one of my making—had gone up between us.

13

Tryst

After returning to the main house, Jaicon went in search of Merrigan while I visited Jada. She had withdrawn further than yesterday, and my concern for her increased. She spoke very little and, shortly after I arrived, slept.

I heard a soft knock at the door, and when it eased open and I saw Zin, I put my finger to my lips and stood to join him in the hallway.

"How is she doing?" he asked.

"Bones gave her something to help her sleep," I explained.

"Doc mentioned you think it would be a good idea for her to visit your ranch."

"Yes."

"He also told me I needed to wait for an invitation to go myself."

I walked farther down the hall, and he followed. "I have not yet broached the subject with Jada. She may not want to go. If she does and she wants you to accompany her, then by all means, you should."

"You don't think she will, though."

"She's withdrawing."

"Doc also mentioned you said the same thing to him."

I motioned to her door. "Go ahead, now. I'll stand watch."

"What do you mean?"

"I will not allow Montano to interfere with your visit."

Zin exhaled. "Thanks, Tryst."

I only saw Onyx briefly when he arrived later in the afternoon, and we did not speak. The turmoil I felt from him seemed to increase proportionately to Jada's withdrawal. Her being here, at Butler Ranch, wasn't a good thing for either of them. However, Bones had not yet released her medically, and until he did, she'd have to remain here or move to another medical facility.

My attempts at meeting up with Jaicon were unsuccessful. Something had shifted during our walk this morning. Without it being said, the subject of children, of having a family, was a dividing factor for us. The idea of her giving up the option at thirty-two years of age seemed tragic. I couldn't ask that of her, which meant we both needed to rethink how deep into a relationship we should go if its ending was inevitable.

Shortly after Sorcha served dinner, I left for the Los Caballeros wine caves, where the emergency meeting was taking place. When I arrived, Brix was waiting for me outside.

"Since it was called by the *viejos*, I think you should lead."

I could see the wisdom in his suggestion and said so. "To my knowledge, tonight is the first time there will be people who are not members in attendance," I added. "However, Laird and Kade are trusted friends of the *caballeros*."

"I agree, Uncle. In deference to our elders, the current members have agreed the *viejos* will be seated and we will stand behind them."

As was our tradition, once we entered the caves, Brix and I did not speak again until the rest of the members arrived. The only *caballero* not present was Beau Barrett. After the passing of his mother last week, he left the States and went to the UK, although his exact whereabouts were not common knowledge.

After making eye contact with each present, also part of the ritual, I began the meeting. "Thank you for joining us, *caballeros*. You have honored us with your presence."

Each of the *viejos* nodded.

"We're here to discuss a breach in the armor of our beloved brotherhood," I continued. "Given the urgency and viability of the threat, as you are all aware, we've asked Burns and Doc Butler to join our meeting."

Both men were invited in and to take a seat. Laird folded his hands on the table. "Thank you for allowing us to participate this evening. I'm afraid the news we're about to deliver is not good." He looked at his son, who spoke next.

"Onyx Yáñez resigned from his position at K19 Security Solutions today."

"May I speak?" Zin asked.

"Of course."

"I am resigning from Los Caballeros, effective immediately."

No one in the room agreed his doing so would help the situation with Onyx. After allowing everyone else who wished to speak to do so, I weighed in. "No one is resigning. However, your actions could have had serious consequences. They still might if Montano Yáñez—Onyx—remains determined we disband." I thought about Tank's earlier question, asking if Zin would face repercussions. In my opinion, the man was in a hell of his own making. The pain and agony he suffered over Jada was punishment enough. I looked over at Burns. "What exactly are we facing?"

"Yáñez has no evidence against Los Caballeros or any of its members."

"Are you certain?" I asked.

"Yes," Kade answered for him.

"What about Al Zaabi's death?" Brix asked.

"Taken care of," Kade responded. "However, my recommendation is that Los Caballeros enter an extended period of inactivity."

"I am in agreement." This would also serve as an atonement of sorts for Zin. He would feel great guilt over putting the *caballeros* at risk.

Before adjourning, I ask Laird, Kade, and the current members to step out of the room.

"Gentlemen, I am opening the floor for discussion."

"We've weathered worse," said Martin Barrett, repeating what he'd said when all were present.

"What about sanctions?" I asked, looking around the room. "Shall we take a vote?"

"Would you like me to leave the room?" asked Michael Oliver, Zin's father.

"No. You will remain."

He nodded.

"All those in favor of sanctions against Vaile Oliver?"

Not a single hand went up.

"Opposed."

The decision was unanimous.

"You have honored the spirit and history of Los Caballeros, my brothers, and I thank you."

It was after midnight when I returned to Angus House and went upstairs. I feared Jaicon would not be waiting in the bed we'd shared the night before, and was greatly relieved to see she was. This time, she was under the bedclothes.

After going through the same routine I had the night before, I crawled in beside her. Her back was to my front, and I put my arm around her waist.

"How did it go?" she whispered without turning to look at me.

"Montano has no evidence against the caballeros."

"Burns worked his magic?"

"Yes."

"I'm glad."

"As am I."

I reached up and stroked her hair. "Sleep, beautiful girl, and we will speak more tomorrow."

While her breathing evened out almost immediately, I lay in the darkness, troubled by the chasm I felt between us. Was it simply that the events of the last two days were more important than what we had? I couldn't explain why it felt like more.

When I woke the following morning, I was alone in bed and the sheets were cold. I checked my phone to see if Jaicon had sent a message and found one from Bones instead, asking me to meet him to talk to Jada. I showered, dressed, and walked over to the main residence.

Bones and I entered Jada's room at the same time, and after telling her he thought she was well enough to be able to leave Butler Ranch, we discussed her options.

As I'd anticipated, her reaction to going to New York with her brother or to her mother's home was negative. Her hesitation to travel with me to *El Lugar de Curación* surprised me.

After asking Bones if she could talk to me alone, she shared the reasons for her reluctance.

"I don't want to impose, Tryst."

"There is no better place for you, little one. It is the Healing Place. While you are not my niece by blood, you called me uncle until you decided you were too old to do so. I think you were thirteen."

She smiled. "I don't want to go home."

I nodded. "Mine is your home too, Jada. You are always welcome."

When she agreed, I told her I'd make the arrangements and left the room, surprised to see Jaicon waiting in the hallway. "Good morning."

She motioned for me to follow, and we went out to the porch. "You were sleeping so peacefully I didn't want to wake you earlier."

"Jada has agreed to travel to my ranch."

She nodded. "I think it's the best place for her."

"I told her I'd make the arrangements."

"I will be traveling there in advance of your arrival. Zeppelin and Magnet will go with me. Since I'm familiar with the ranch's security protocols, the three of us will ensure everything we need is in place. Unless you have a reason to believe they should stay, they'll then return to the UK."

"I am in agreement. It will not be necessary for them to remain."

"Good. I'll set everything up on my end." She turned to leave.

"Jacy?"

"I'll see you in Mexico, Tryst."

14

Jaicon

Tryst didn't try to stop me as I rushed from the house, nor did he follow. As much as I wanted to explain, I couldn't. Not until I had answers for myself.

Last night, while he was at the emergency meeting of Los Caballeros, I'd drifted off while waiting for him to get back and dreamed about my dead husband, but not him alone.

I woke, gripping one of the pillows on the bed where I'd been resting, hugging it close to my body, as if its softness would somehow ease the excruciating pain I'd feel as the memories of the night Edmund "Banker" Codd died raced through my head.

The car that careened into the passenger side of ours came out of nowhere, traveling at a speed that had to be greater than sixty kilometers per hour. Its head- and taillights were as dark as the vehicle itself, so I hadn't seen it coming or going.

The images of it sideswiping us and our car spinning out of control and into a ravine were replaced with those of my husband as blood dripped from his nose and mouth. His breath gurgled with it as I placed a call for emergency services, begging them to hurry but knowing, deep inside, in less than a few more heartbeats, it would be too late to save him.

Edmund's eyes bored into mine as the realization he had seconds to live hit him. I cupped his cheek, tears pouring from my eyes, as I told him I loved him and begged him to hold on.

He said only one word before life left him. *Love.* My keening filled the silence of the night as I waited for emergency medical services while clinging to my dead husband.

Knowing I had little choice, I let the rest of the night's events play themselves out inside my head—the EMTs removing me from the vehicle and transporting me to the hospital, where the attending physicians informed me of both my losses. My parents were with me when they confirmed what I already knew about Edmund. My other loss was the baby I'd only told him I carried that night.

That was the most heartbreaking part of the dream. In his arms, Edmund held a little towheaded girl who looked a lot like me when I was three years old. "Mama?" she'd said, reaching for me just as I woke up.

Listening to Tryst talk about how he and his wife hadn't explored their issues with fertility after her diagnosis, was a reminder that I had no idea whether I could have more children. After Edmund's death, I hadn't had a reason to find out. I still didn't.

I was gathering the few belongings I'd unpacked when I heard a knock at the cottage's door.

"Hey," I said, opening it and waving Merrigan inside.

"How are you doing, Jacy?"

I studied her. "What makes you ask?"

"I saw you with Tryst earlier. You appeared upset."

"I need to pack." When I went up the stairs, Merrigan followed.

"What happened?"

"I dreamed about Edmund last night. And the baby." Merrigan was the only other person I'd told how much more I lost the night of Edmund's death. When I sat on the edge of the bed, she sat beside me.

"I'm so sorry."

"I know you are. Everyone is. It was a tragic event. The most painful of my life. And just when I start—"

I couldn't continue. Had I really expected to *move on*? Had I truly believed a relationship with any man, let alone Tryst Avila, was possible?

"Jaicon, I beg you not to let go of this thing with Tryst. You are both entitled to experience love and happiness again. There are no two people more deserving of it."

I shook my head. "It doesn't matter how many days, weeks, months, or years pass. For the rest of my life, I will wake in the throes of a nightmare about the accident that will result in its entirety playing out in vivid detail. Tryst is not deserving of such an experience."

"Would you deny him comfort if something reminds him of the loss of his wife?"

She knew I would not. "Zeppelin and Magnet are waiting. They're traveling with me to Alamos in advance of Tryst's arrival with Jada."

"Jaicon—"

"Merrigan, I love you dearly, but I do not want to talk about Edmund, the accident, or Tryst as he relates to anything other than a consultant I'm working with in order to help facilitate an investigation into who is ultimately behind Luisa Reeve's abduction and the sex-slave-auction site she was found on."

"Is that the only way you see him now? I had the impression the two of you had grown close."

I shook my head, blinking my eyes against the tears that threatened. "The dream I had last night served as a reminder that I'm not ready to move on, to act as if I didn't lose the love of my life or our child. If anything, it was good I realized it before I'd become more attached to Tryst."

"What about him? He has no say? No right to know the decision you've made that will also affect him?"

"Your supposition that I would not show him that courtesy belies the friendship I believe we have."

She put her hand on my arm. "You're right, and I apologize. I do know better than to think you could be so callous."

"If you truly are my friend, truly care about me, you'll not push me into something I'm not ready for."

"While it breaks my heart to see you walk away from another chance at love, I give you my word that I will not push."

"Thank you. Now, I really do need to go."

We stood and embraced. "Please remember I am always here whenever you need me. Even when you don't."

I smiled. "I know."

Zeppelin and Magnet took turns sitting in the cockpit of the Cirrus Vision with me on the trip from the airfield in San Luis Obispo to Tryst's ranch. Each feigned enthusiasm over the aircraft's design and the view, but it was evident neither wanted to leave me alone. It was somewhat amusing in that if something had gone wrong, neither man would be able to fly the plane.

"This place is brilliant," said Zep after we taxied and I maneuvered away from the runway. I wasn't surprised to see a golf cart parked and waiting for us. In it was a note indicating the two men with me had their choice of *casitas* and that the staff would provide anything they or I needed.

"I understand why everyone loves coming here," added Magnet.

"It is quite magical, and you haven't seen all of it yet."

On the way to the *casita* where I'd stayed previously, we passed by the meditation center. When we reached the barns and I saw Tex working with Cariño, I asked the guys if they'd mind if we stopped.

The three of us climbed on the fence rail and watched. I saw signs of her skittishness every so often, but she was doing so much better. I was astounded. She'd put on weight, and her coat shined beautifully.

"When that horse arrived at the rehabilitation center, she was in terrible condition. The progress they've made with her is remarkable." I'd kept my voice low when I made the comment to Zep and Mag, but evidently not low enough for Cariño not to hear.

Tex laughed when she pulled away, straining the catch rope. He quickly released her, and she came bounding over to the fence.

"She's happy to see you!" Tex shouted.

"Likewise. She looks fantastic." The horse pushed at me with her nose, and I scratched behind her ears. "I've missed you, girl," I whispered. She responded with a soft nicker.

She stiffened when Tex approached, but once he jumped up on the fence with the others, she settled. "I was going to see how she took to a saddle in the next couple of days. Would you like to be here when I do?"

"I would love to be," I said, but then thought better of it. "I am working, Tex. So as much as I do, it will depend on what else is going on."

He nodded. "I spoke with Tryst earlier. He filled me in."

"Then you understand that while I may want to stay and watch, the things we need to do in advance of his arrival take priority."

"Copy that, Jacy. Good to see you back here."

"What's that?" asked Zep once we'd returned to the golf cart and were en route to the *casitas*. I shielded my eyes from the sun and looked where he pointed.

"I believe it's a temple. I've not visited." It dawned on me it was the one place on the ranch Tryst had never taken me to. I couldn't help but wonder why he hadn't.

15

Tryst

My concern for both Jada and Jaicon weighed heavily on me. While the former's need for comfort and healing appeared to be the more urgent of the two, I couldn't help but think I had somehow let Jaicon down.

I thought through our last few interactions many times and couldn't pinpoint exactly when things had shifted as drastically as they had.

Nothing I could recall saying in the conversation we'd had about children was something I believed would have hurt her. Yet, that was when things had changed between us.

I replayed what I'd said about Rosa being diagnosed with cancer after we sought advice about fertility in my head and did my best to recall her reaction, and still, nothing explained her withdrawal. She'd said she understood.

After that, I'd asked whether she and her husband had discussed having a family, and she'd responded they had not.

I also thought about holding her in my arms last night. It had felt different than the night before.

Rather than looking for what might have upset her, perhaps I should turn my gaze inward. Was it me who was feeling so unsettled? Was I projecting my own issues onto her?

There was only one thing I was certain of, and that was as soon as I could, I needed to visit the meditation center so I could figure this out.

It was almost midnight by the time Jada was settled enough I felt as though I could leave her alone with Lynne, the nurse who had traveled with us.

The air outside was chilled, but the moon was bright as I drove from my house to the place I knew would soothe my soul more than any other.

When I got closer, I was surprised to see another cart parked in front, as well as the glow of candlelight from inside. I thought about turning around and leaving whoever it was in peace, but curiosity and my own need to meditate compelled me to stay.

I thanked the gods and goddesses when I peeked in the window and saw it was Jaicon. There wasn't anyone I needed to feel a connection with more than her.

I entered the space as quietly as I could but came to a dead stop when I heard her sobbing. She sat in Siddhasana pose, facing the *mandir*, and when I went to step closer, it was as though my ankles were shackled.

From the time the center was first built, I'd never felt like I didn't belong here. Until tonight. I felt like I was intruding on something private—something Jaicon didn't want me to see or hear. I took several steps backwards and left as quietly as I'd come.

When I woke the next morning, I was as tired as when I'd gone to bed. I missed the comfort of sleeping beside Jaicon, but thinking about sleeping with her here now, even without intimacy, felt wrong.

"Good morning," said Lynne, joining me in the kitchen as I stared into a cup of black coffee. "I'm not sure who had a harder night, you or Jada."

I looked up at her. "What happened?"

"Nightmares woke her several times. After a while, I just stayed in the room with her. Then she seemed to rest easier."

"She felt your presence."

"I think you're right." Lynne sat in the chair opposite mine. "What about you, Tryst?"

"I am unsettled."

"That's obvious."

I smiled, appreciating the direct approach of the woman who hailed from Brooklyn.

"Hi," said Jada, padding into the room.

"Good morning, little one," I said, standing and pulling out a chair at the table. "Coffee?"

"Bless you," she responded, taking the seat I offered.

"How's your pain this morning?" I heard Lynne ask while I fetched a cup. I didn't hear what else either said, but when I turned around, Lynne had left the room.

"She's nice," Jada said when I set the coffee in front of her along with cream and sugar. "You used to call me little one when I was a child. I'd forgotten."

"You were very small."

"Onyx used to call me the runt."

"Oral or IM?" Lynne asked when she returned to the kitchen.

Like a few minutes ago, the women's voices faded as my thoughts returned to Jaicon. I somehow knew her tears last night were not for me. Perhaps that was what had stopped me from approaching her. On the other hand, why hadn't I been able to reach out to comfort her, even in friendship? I shook my head, feeling unlike myself.

I stood and looked out the window in the direction of the *casita* where I knew she'd spent the night. I'd lingered in the darkness after I returned from the meditation center until I saw the lights of the golf cart approach and watched her go inside.

I'd known she was safe before that. I'd asked one of the men who worked security on the ranch to monitor the video feeds.

"There is a guest at the meditation center," I'd said when he answered my call.

"I have my eye on her," he responded. "I've got a couple of my guys posted nearby. No one will bother her," he assured me.

I still remained awake until I was certain of it myself.

"Don't be too tough on yourself now, when it isn't necessary," I heard Lynne say to Jada before leaving the room a second time.

"I agree," I said. "There is no timeline for healing. Take it as it comes, and do not push yourself unnecessarily."

She rested her chin in her hand. "I just want to get out of my head for a while."

"When you're ready, we'll visit the meditation center. It will be a good place for you to do so."

"Ready today or ready another time?"

I smiled. "When you're ready."

"The medication made me sleepy."

"Then, you should rest."

When Jada got up from the table, she leaned over and kissed my temple. "Thank you for bringing me here, Tryst."

"You are my family, Jada. As I said before, my home is yours as well."

After she left the room, I went out to the *terraza*. After a few minutes, Jaicon came outside too.

"Good morning," I said, raising my cup of coffee in her direction.

"Good morning, Tryst."

I walked closer and sat on the stone wall surrounding the enclosed area. "How are you, Jaicon?"

She turned to me but didn't respond for several seconds. "You already know how I am."

"Do I?"

She nodded, looking off in the distance. "I knew you were there last night."

"I am sorry for intruding."

"You didn't. You left. Why?"

"I cannot tell you. I felt as though I shouldn't be there."

"I see."

"Jaicon, I would very much like for us to talk."

Her gaze met mine. "I would too. Maybe this afternoon?"

"I will come to you."

She turned to go inside.

"Jacy?"

"I'll see you later, Tryst."

Midafternoon, right before I planned to walk over to visit Jaicon, Jada came out of the bedroom, saying she was ready to go to the meditation center. Two hours later, everything went to hell.

"What can I do?" Lynne asked when she opened the door and I swept inside with Jada in my arms. Maria, one of the women who worked on the ranch, raced in behind us.

"Help us get her out of these clothes and into a warm bath," I said, sitting on the bed while still holding Jada in my arms.

"She's past due for her pain meds. I'll be right back."

Once Lynne returned and gave Jada the medication, she closed her eyes and fell into a deep sleep.

"We'll take it from here," Lynne said when I eased her from my arms and onto the bed. "You look like you could use a drink." She guided me out of the room. "We've got this, Tryst."

The sun had set, and it was dark, but I did not turn a light on. Instead, I sat in a chair, put my head in my hands, and wept.

Several minutes later, I heard the two women come out of Jada's room. "Tryst?" Lynne called out.

"I'm here." I stood, hit the light switch, and called out my thanks to Maria when she walked out the front door.

"What happened this afternoon?" Lynne asked.

I motioned for her to take a seat, but she shook her head. "I need to listen in case she wakes up."

"Understood." I sighed and closed my eyes. "She heard the sound of a whip. It triggered her. I should've known. I should've anticipated it." I raked my hands through my hair.

"Hang on. Slow down. A whip?"

"They are used at the riding center, but not in the way you might think. I tried to explain it to Jada, but she was too far gone by then."

I jumped when I heard Jada whimper. "Let me," I said when Lynne walked in the direction of the bedroom. "I want to stay with her."

Her eyes scrunched, but she nodded. "I'll be across the hallway if you need me."

When I felt a hand on my shoulder, I scrubbed my face with my palm and opened my eyes. It was daylight.

"Please go get some sleep," said Jada.

"How are you this morning?" I asked, slowly attempting to loosen my muscles, stiff and sore from sleeping in the chair.

"Better. I'm sorry about yesterday."

I leaned down and kissed her forehead. "Do not apologize."

"I lost it."

"It is part of the process, little one. The fault is mine." I looked over at Lynne. "Will you be okay if I sleep a while?"

"I'll kick your butt if you don't."

I was on my way into my bedroom when Lynne opened Jada's door. "Before I forget again, Jaicon stopped by yesterday. I told her you and Jada were at the meditation center. Did she find you?"

My God, I'd completely forgotten I told her we'd talk yesterday. "She did not," I said, shaking my head.

"Get some rest, Tryst."

I sat on the edge of the bed and called Jaicon. It immediately went to voicemail, so I sent a text.

I'm sorry about yesterday. Jada had a setback. Please call when you receive this message.

I lay down and shut my eyes but held my phone in my hand in case she responded. When I woke a few hours later, she hadn't.

Jada and Lynne were sitting in the kitchen when I came out of the bedroom.

"Did you get some rest?" Jada asked.

"I did." I turned to Lynne. "Will you excuse us?"

"Are you okay?" Jada asked once the nurse left the room.

I was not. I owed her an apology. "I'm sorry for pushing you yesterday. I was the one who told you there is no timeline to healing."

"You're wrong now. You weren't then."

My eyes scrunched.

"If you don't push me, who will?"

"The progress you make, working through your recovery, will be up to you, little one."

"Will you take me to the meditation center?"

My eyes opened wide. "When?"

"Now?"

I smiled. "Are you certain you wouldn't rather wait a few days?"

She shook her head. "You said something yesterday about the context of how the whips I heard were used."

"Yes."

"How are they used, Tryst?"

"When you are ready, it will be better for you to see."

"You won't tell me?"

"I will not."

"Then, I want to see it."

Jada and I sat on the hillside, watching as Tex led Cariño into the corral.

"The demonstration will begin very soon."

"Of what?" she asked.

"Trust."

"It involves the whip, doesn't it?"

I stood and held out my hand to her. "Come, we'll be on our way."

"I told you I want to do this."

"It was the sound of the whip that affected you so profoundly yesterday, little one."

"You said it was something I had to see to understand. I want to."

"If it is too much—"

"You said they aren't used on the horses."

"They are not. I promise you. They are not used to hit anything at all." I pointed again. "Watch the cowboy."

While Jada watched Tex, my gaze was focused on Jaicon, who stood on the opposite side of the corral, watching just as intently.

Tex threw his leg over the horse, then pushed himself onto his feet, balancing as he stood on the saddle.

"Keep your eyes on him," I said to Jada.

When Tex cracked the whip, the tail of the leather hit the dirt. Cariño didn't flinch. He continued, shifting the direction he faced by slowly shuffling his feet, then cracking the whip again.

"When the horse arrived at the ranch, she was severely malnourished. She'd been horribly abused for years," I explained.

"Whipped?" Jada asked.

"Yes, but now, she no longer fears she'll be hurt. She trusts."

Tex lowered himself to a sitting position and maneuvered the horse over to the corral's gate. When it opened, Jaicon approached them and he handed her the reins. With her opposite hand, she wiped her face, then mounted and took Cariño through several paces in the enclosed area.

"Does she belong to her?" Jada asked.

Even with the distance separating us, I knew when Jaicon's eyes met mine. When I raised my hand and waved, she looked away.

"She may one day soon." While I said I believed she might, I responded she would more out of hope than the belief it would happen.

"She means something to you, doesn't she?"

"She does, little one."

"You should tell her that."

"You are right, and I will." I only wished I didn't feel as though it was already too late.

Over the course of the next two weeks, I saw little of Jaicon. The investigation into the deaths of the two men in La Higuera as well as into the sex-slave auction where Luisa Reeve's photo still appeared necessitated she travel regularly to California. As much as I wanted to assist, I did not feel comfortable leaving Jada.

Each time we spoke of it, Jaicon assured me she understood and encouraged me to continue making Jada my priority. At the same time, she was cool and aloof, widening the chasm I already felt between us.

It was hard to imagine there had been a time we felt comfortable enough to sleep in each other's arms, or lost ourselves in fantasies and kisses.

"Hello, Brix," I said, pleased to see he was calling. "How's Jada?"

"She has good days and bad, but that is to be expected. How is Addy?"

"The morning sickness is better. She attributes it to being here in Mexico."

"I cannot tell you how happy that makes me. Do you think she would feel well enough for the two of you to join us for dinner?"

"I'll ask, but I'm sure she'll say she'd enjoy it very much."

"This evening?"

"That sounds great, Tryst. We'll see you around six."

When our call ended, I felt more like myself than I had in days. So much so, I called Jaicon to invite her to join us.

I was further elated when she graciously accepted and said she looked forward to it.

I went about my day, prepping food for our meal.

"You're in a good mood today," said Lynne when she came into the kitchen a couple of hours later.

"I have invited my nephew and his wife, as well as Jaicon, to join us for dinner this evening."

"The normalcy will do Jada good. You too, obviously."

As always, I appreciated her frankness.

Unfortunately, the evening did not go as planned. While I enjoyed the time with Brix and Addy very much, Jada was more withdrawn than she had been in the last few days. And, at the last minute, Jaicon canceled, citing an urgent trip to California.

When Lynne and Addy insisted they clean up after the meal, Brix and I went outside to light the *chimenea*.

"I realized earlier I asked about Jada, but I neglected to ask about you, Tryst."

"I am the same as I always am, nephew."

He shook his head. "No, you are not, and don't say it's because of Jada. Something else is going on with you."

I glanced in the direction of the *casita* next door, sad to find it dark, but also relieved that Jaicon had been honest about having to go to California.

"What happened between the two of you?" he asked.

"I wish I knew."

Brix shook his head. "It isn't like you to give up so easily."

There was nothing easy about it. There were days I fretted about what had gone wrong and others I agonized.

"Tryst?"

"I'm sorry, Brix. If I had the answers you seek, we would not be having this conversation."

16

Tryst

The following morning, I was awakened from a deep sleep by a call from the barns. There was an emergency they needed my help with. One of the horses that was out in the pasture had gotten tangled in fencing and was believed to have a broken leg.

I raced from the house, and rather than take the golf cart, I drove the four-wheeler I kept in one of the outbuildings that would get me over the rugged terrain more easily.

"Which horse is it?" I asked Tex via walkie-talkie as I drove out.

"It's Berta, Tryst."

My heart sank. Berta was a horse Jada had connected with almost immediately upon her arrival at the ranch. She rode her almost daily, and the two had formed a tight bond. That she had been injured and would likely need to be put down would be devastating.

When I reached the pasture, I was stunned to see Zin standing beside my nephew.

"Before you say anything, I invited him here several days ago. He's been helping me with the house."

I glared at Brix before walking over to the vet, who was examining Berta. "We have more urgent matters to attend to at this time."

"We're here to help, Tryst. Just let us know what we can do."

"It doesn't look good," said David, the veterinarian who cared for all of the horses at the riding center. "She must've been attacked by coyotes, and it spooked her enough for her to get tangled up in the fence."

I soothed the horse Jada had nicknamed B. "What can be done?" I asked.

"We can try to X-ray the leg, then determine what to do next."

"Let's." I raised my head when I heard a woman screaming.

"Wait!" It was Jada, and she was astride Cariño.

"Back away and give her space," I said when she got closer. While I knew she'd seen Zin, her primary concern was Berta. Even I stood and stepped away to allow her to comfort the animal.

"I'm going to sedate her so we can get her back to the barn," said David, stepping forward with a syringe.

"No! Not yet!" Jada screamed.

Before I could do so myself, Zin stepped forward. "He's just going to sedate her so we can get her back to the barn without further injury. That's all, Jada."

She looked up at me, and I nodded.

Tex arrived in the pickup, and those of us there rolled B onto a stretcher, then hefted her into the back of the pickup. When it pulled away, Jada was seated in the flatbed with her.

"Tryst—"

"Not now, Brix." I hadn't yet decided how I felt about Zin being here when I'd specifically said that until Jada asked for him, he should not come. Until I sorted out my feelings, I wouldn't be prepared to talk to either man.

When I reached the barns, I overheard Jada saying, "She's not going to be put down," to the vet.

I rested my hand on her shoulder. As in all things, I could not lie to her. "If that's what is best for her, that is what we will do. We cannot allow Berta to endlessly suffer, little one."

After returning with the portable X-ray machine, David determined the break was not as bad as he'd feared. He suggested putting a cast on it and waiting to see how it healed. The recovery would not be easy since Berta would not be able to put weight on it.

As I was leaving the barn, Jada approached me.

"Tryst, did you know Zin was here?" She had asked me a couple of days ago, and I'd assured her he wasn't. Evidently, she'd sensed his presence then.

"Not until earlier, when he and Brix showed up in the pasture. When you asked, I didn't know he'd come with my nephew. I would not lie to you, Jada."

Now that he was here, I attempted to give Zin and Jada a wide berth, but the tension between them was evident. I found myself avoiding the barns and even the meditation center. Instead, I most often visited the chapel. That is where I was when I received a call from Montano.

"Hey, Tryst, is there someone here who can sit with Berta? Jada needs to leave the barn."

"Of course," I said. "There are several hands available to do so. Ask any one of them. Wait. Are you here, at the ranch?"

"Yeah, uh, Press and I flew down."

Something told me nothing was as simple as it sounded. "I will meet you at the house."

I'd just arrived and he and I were chatting when Jada came flying out of the bedroom.

"Where is Zin?" she demanded.

I looked from her brother to her, not knowing how to respond.

"Don't pretend like you don't know. Lynne just told me you took him to the hospital."

I had no idea what she was talking about.

"I didn't say he did. One of the cowboys swung by here, looking for him," said Lynne, who looked over at me. "You, I mean."

"I just returned."

"Can you find out which hospital?" Jada asked.

I stood. "There is only one. I will take you."

I waited in the truck while Jada spoke to her brother.

"What happened?" I asked once we were on our way.

"Montano caught us, uh, fooling around. He punched Zin. Again."

I looked over at her with a raised brow.

"Come on. I've been seeing him for four years. You couldn't have thought I meant anything other than having sex."

I smiled and shook my head.

"I'm a grown woman," she muttered.

"You will not get any argument from me. And just so you know, I'm happy to hear you were, uh, fooling around."

When we arrived at the hospital, Zin and Press were coming out the front entrance. I waited when Jada got out to speak with them.

"They're going to follow us to the ranch," she said a few minutes later.

"Can I give you some uncley advice?" I asked after we'd been driving a few minutes.

"Sure."

"I speak from experience, little one. Be honest. Tell Zin how you truly feel. Do not make the mistakes I have. Do not lose this chance for love."

When she asked if I meant mistakes with Rosa, I shook my head. However, I wasn't prepared to talk to Jada, or anyone else, about Jaicon. It wasn't until this very moment that I realized how deeply the loss of her in my life had affected me.

My days became a never-ending cycle of worry about Berta, Jada, Jaicon, and even Cariño, who Tex said had had a setback in her recovery.

Sadly, I continued to avoid the meditation center in particular. It had always been a place of solace for me, and since the night I came upon Jaicon there, sobbing, I'd been filled with guilt about not comforting her.

A week to the day since the last time she and I spoke, I'd just entered the barn to let Jada know the vet was here to check on Berta when Jaicon walked in.

After she said hello to Jada, I asked if I could speak with her privately.

We walked out of the barn, and I led her over to the corral. As it so happened, Tex was there with Cariño.

"She's doing so well. You should be very proud of the work you do here."

"Jacy, I want you to know how sorry I am about the other day. I promised we'd talk, and then—"

"Please do not apologize. I understand Jada is your first priority."

I closed my eyes and lifted my face to the sun. Was that the way she saw it? Was that the way it was? I opened my eyes and looked into hers. "Jada is one priority, not necessarily my first."

"She needs you. I think I understand better than anyone."

"What makes you say it in that way?" I asked.

"When my husband died, the accident…Merrigan was there for me. She comforted me, helped me deal with the pain in ways my parents couldn't, even though they really wanted to."

"I miss you, Jaicon. I miss the time we spent together so much. When you had to cancel dinner—"

Jacy sighed. "I told you I was sorry, Tryst, but I had to go to California. I'm here to do a job. Not…"

"Not what?" I asked.

"Not get involved."

"I wish I knew what happened between us. I wish I understood where I went wrong."

She folded her arms. "You didn't. Things went the way they were supposed to. While we may have both believed we wanted something romantic to develop, you have to admit that neither of us is truly ready for that. Thankfully, it ended before it began, saving us both the inevitable heartache."

I thought back to the day she said we were both to "blame" for the kiss we'd shared. Today's words hurt just as bad as that had. "I'm sorry—"

"Tryst, don't. There's nothing to be sorry for. We're work colleagues and friends. At least, I hope we are."

"We are. You are very special to me, Jaicon."

"As you are to me." She looked at her watch. "I need to go. I came to tell you my help is needed in the UK and I may be gone for an extended period of time."

I raised a brow. "The UK?"

"The mandate of the K19 team I command is to provide support for international missions," she said, as if that somehow explained why she'd be gone a lengthy amount of time.

"What about the investigation into the deaths of the men tied to Manual Varilla?"

"There are no leads presently. If that changes, I'll return. Goodbye, Tryst."

I watched her walk away until she was out of my line of sight. Waiting, hoping, praying she'd turn and look. She did not.

17

Tryst

I was working in the barn the next day when I smelled the smoke and heard shouts of "Fire!" simultaneously. I raced outside.

"It's the meditation center!" someone shouted.

"No!" I cried, running as fast as my feet would carry me. The flames engulfed my beloved building, burning it to the ground before the first water truck arrived.

"Oh my God!" I spun around to see Zin racing toward me. The look of panic on his face sent me into a rage.

"What did you do?" I shouted.

"I don't know what happened. I was looking for Jada—"

"You fucking *sonuvabitch*. You burned down my Rosa's meditation center," I yelled.

"I didn't. There was a coyote. I threw my phone." He broke down. "God, Tryst, I'm so sorry. It was an accident. I swear it."

I couldn't look at him. I could hardly speak. "Get off my property," I seethed. "You are no longer welcome here."

There was no indication of the passage of time as I sat in the grass, staring at the scorched earth where the place I'd built to honor my beloved wife used to stand. I alternated between uncontrollable weeping and wild anger, raging at the deities who'd allowed this to happen, but stopping short of cursing God.

"Tryst?" I heard my nephew call out.

I wished to hide, to become invisible, to let my feelings play out without a witness, but that would not be fair to Brix. I had no doubt he was as sick with worry as I would be if the situations were reversed. "I'm here," I said, raising an arm.

He approached, sat on the grass beside me, and put his arms around me. "I'm so sorry, Tryst. I'm just so fucking sorry." He and I wept together.

"What happened? Do you know? Zin said it was an accident."

"I cannot speak or hear of it."

He nodded once. "I understand. You do know Jada left, right?"

"Yes." It was something else I couldn't speak of. My worry for her was the only thing that came close to matching the intensity of my sorrow.

He looked up at the sky. "Calm before the storm, Tryst. We need to find cover."

He stood and held his hand out to me, helping me to my feet. "Go home, Brix. Go be with Addy. Hold her close and tell her how much you love her."

"What will you do?" he asked, worry etched on his face.

"I will find my way."

"I don't want you to go out in the storm."

"I will not be. I promise you as much."

I made it to the barns before the storm hit and walked over to Cariño's stall. While she had improved so much the horse was hardly recognizable, I knew the thunder would frighten her. I held out my hand, and when she raised her head, I opened the door and went inside. I rested my cheek against her neck and cried.

"Tryst, are you in here?" I heard Tex holler several minutes later.

I wiped my tears and exited the stall. "What's happened now?" I asked.

"Can you come look at this?"

I followed him into the office, where there was a set of security monitors.

"See that?" He pointed to one of the screens.

The rain was torrential, and it was hard to see anything beyond it. "What is it?" I asked.

He paused the recording and rewound it. I watched as a man I recognized as Zin came out of the woods and made his way to the area behind where the meditation center used to stand. He picked something up, then walked over and sat on the ground against a tree.

"You want me to send someone out for him, Tryst? He's gonna get himself electrocuted."

I shook my head. "I'll take care of it." I got in my truck and drove as close as I could get to him. The rain was coming down harder and getting worse as I raced over to where he sat. His head was down when I put my hand on his shoulder, then held it out to help him up.

"I'm on my way to check on Berta," I said once we were in the truck and out of the rain.

We didn't speak again until we reached the vet's office. I pulled a jacket from behind the seat and handed it to him. "Put this on," I said before going inside, where the vet waited.

"She'll be glad to see the two of you," he said as we followed him into the back.

"Go ahead," I said, motioning Zin into where Berta rested. I handed him a face brush and turned to leave when I heard him ask me to stay.

When I hesitated, he said, "She needs both of us." With Jada gone, I agreed. In fact, we all needed each other, even though I was too angry to say it.

When we returned, I dropped him off at Brix's place. "We'll go again tomorrow," I said when he got out.

When I arrived at the burn scar two days later, I was stunned to see a group of people already hard at work, clearing the debris.

"What is this?" I asked when George Norman and Malcolm Warwick approached me.

"This is what Los Caballeros does, Tryst. We show up when we're needed," said George, putting his hand on my shoulder. "I heard you could use an architect."

I raised a brow.

"Come with me, and I'll show you what I've drawn up for the rebuild."

"The rebuild?"

"Yes, Tryst," said Malcolm. "We aren't leaving until it's completed."

With the exception of Press, all the *caballeros* who were at the emergency meeting almost three weeks ago showed up to help. Their presence and generosity moved me to tears many times. Forty-eight hours ago, I thought nothing in the world could lift my spirits—other than seeing Jaicon again. Not that I knew when I would. Two days after she left, Atticus showed up, saying he'd be filling in for her until she could return from the UK. When I asked him when that would be, he said he had no idea.

Whenever I thought of her, I thought of my Rosa, wondering if Jaicon had been correct when she said things between us had gone the way they were supposed to. "While we may have both believed we wanted something romantic to develop, you have to admit that neither of us is truly ready for that," she'd said.

Rosa was my one great and true love, and I'd vowed to honor her every day for the rest of my life and forever, into eternity. Had my desire for Jaicon been a betrayal of that vow? Laird had said my late wife wouldn't have wanted me to live the rest of my life without love, but that's where he got it wrong. For the rest of my life, I *would* love. I'd love my Rosa.

I looked over to Zin, who stood with George as he was reviewing the changes I'd requested in the building's design.

Today, he and I would visit Berta one last time before she moved on to a new home. Somewhere she'd be given the time, attention, and love she needed. I would miss her, and Zin would feel her loss just as much.

"We're going to raise the foundation," I heard George say when I approached. "The previous structure was built on a concrete pad. By reinforcing it the way we intend, it will allow us to add heat beneath the floor as well as provide better comfort in other ways."

"What are these?" Zin asked, pointing to the two rooms I'd requested George add.

"Sacred rooms," I responded. "You and I will be the only two working on their construction." I walked away but looked over my shoulder when I realized Zin wasn't following. "It's time to visit Berta. Let's go."

Saying goodbye to Jada's beloved horse was harder than I imagined it would be. When the day came I had to do the same with Cariño, who I would always consider to be Jaicon's, I would be devastated.

With the number of people working tirelessly at rebuilding the meditation center, one week later, everything but the sacred rooms was complete.

I walked to the temple, as I did every day now, and gave thanks for the love and friendship I had in my life rather than mourn what was missing. I'd been there a few minutes when Zin walked in, carrying the plans I'd asked George to give him.

He set the rolls on a pew when I motioned for him to join me. The two of us stood facing the *mandir*.

"I owe you an apology," I began.

"Tryst, please—"

"Allow me to finish. I have been struggling for some time now with my own feelings of betrayal. I made a vow to Rosa that I have not kept. For that, I am filled with regret. More, I am ashamed. What you experienced was anger at myself directed at you. It was unfair—wrong—of me."

"Can I speak now?"

"By all means."

"While the fire was an accident, my actions, my anger, caused it, and I take full responsibility. I know I can never make it up to you, Tryst. Please just know how sorry I am."

"I forgive you, Vaile. Now, you must forgive yourself. That is the hardest part—forgiving ourselves."

"It is."

"I believe there is a way to make it easier for both of us." I walked over to the pew and unfurled the papers. "These are the sacred rooms I asked to be included in the new center. One will be named for Rosa. The other is up to you. We will work together on them. Just the two of us and only when the others have finished for the day."

"Okay."

"Spend the next few hours, days if you need to, meditating on what you would include in the room in order to honor the person whose name you choose."

I remained silent for several minutes, allowing Zin to process everything I'd said. What I'd asked George to do was a gift to both of us. It would enable us to honor the women we loved and, in doing so, find the forgiveness we sought. I prayed for both our souls that it would work.

"The hardest day of my life was when I had to say goodbye to my Rosa. Part of me wanted to go with her, and part of me wanted to beg her not to go. She had to. She'd been hanging on for me, and that wasn't fair. I loved her enough to finally realize I had to let her go."

"I need a few minutes," he said when I walked toward the door.

"Take all the time you need, son."

The first thing I did when I set about creating Rosa's sacred room, her *puja*, was to hang ten *garuda* bells. The significance of placing so many, as opposed to one, which was more common in Hindu temples, was to bring harmony.

Crafted with several types of metals and alloys, it created balance between the left and right hemispheres of the brain, bringing a state of supreme calm when ringing the exact combination.

The purpose of ringing them upon entering a temple or other sacred place was manifold.

First was to put the mind in a state of awareness, ready for prayer. The sound's effect on the brain was to vastly increase the power of concentration.

The subsequent echoes touched the seven chakras of the body—the crown, third eye, throat, heart, solar plexus, sacral, and root—thus relaxing every part of the body.

Finally, the practice warded off negative energy and alerted the gods and deities to accept worship and prayer.

Over the course of several days, I constructed a wooden *mandir*—or Hindu-style altar—made of a combination of rose- and teakwood. It was four feet wide, ten feet tall, and one and a half feet deep, large enough to completely cover one wall of the room.

Its design included one main shelf on top of two drawers flanked by two small cabinets. The most time-consuming aspect of the construction was hand-carving the decorative trim for the front of the storage areas as well as for the symbolic *gopuram*, the pyramid-shaped top section of a temple, or in this case, of the *mandir*.

While completing the carving, I gave a great deal of thought to whether I wanted to paint the piece or leave it with a wood finish. My Rosa had loved the vibrant colors so common in Mexican interior design, so I incorporated a combination of those with traditional Hindu symbolism. I chose hues of bright gold, red, blue, and green.

Once the *mandir* was finished, I hung the artwork I'd created using similar colors to honor Mahadevi, the Mother Goddess. Simply, it was her mantra, written in Sanskrit. Its English translation was, "She is the most auspicious one and the one who bestows auspiciousness upon all of the world. She is pure and holy. She protects those who surrender to her and is also called the Mother of the three worlds and is Gauri, daughter of the mountain king. We bow down to Mother Goddess again and again. We worship her."

The last thing I did—or what I believed would be last—was to place the *mūrtis*, or sculptures, of the deities.

Prominent in the center was Mahadevi. I hadn't decided which other gods to include but was considering Lakshmi, the goddess of power and beauty and Parvati, the goddess of love and marriage. When

I settled on Saraswati, the goddess of creativity and music, who had been one of my Rosa's favorites, the sculpture broke apart in my hands before I could set it on the *mandir*.

As was Hindu custom, I immediately removed the *mūrti* from the room. When I returned, I sat on the heated wooden floor and prayed.

"What am I not seeing, Rosa?" I finally cried when, after what felt like hours of meditation, I still had no clarity. Instead, my heart and soul ached.

Ten days after Zin and I began working on the sacred rooms, he came to me to say he was finished and would be leaving Mexico.

"I want to thank you, Tryst, from the bottom of my heart, for everything you've done for me and for Jada," he said when we walked outside the rebuilt meditation center.

"You are welcome here anytime, Vaile."

He turned to face the temple when his eyes filled with tears. "I'm still working on forgiving myself."

I put my hand on his shoulder. "As am I, son."

After he left, I walked to the hillside where two significant things had happened in my life. First, it was where I stood with my Rosa on the day we met and I promised that, eventually, the land beneath our feet would be our home.

Second was when I took Jaicon to the same place and we'd watched the sunset. I'd told her, then, I felt as though she could use some magic. Instead, as I thought back on it, I was the one who had needed it.

I'd gone too many years without it in my life, and from the first moment I met Jaicon, I knew she'd brought it back to me. Now, it was gone again, and in its wake, I was left unsettled. Even after Rosa was diagnosed, throughout her cancer battle, and after her passing, I did not feel as lost as I had since Jaicon left for the UK nineteen days ago.

I couldn't explain why, but I somehow sensed Jaicon was feeling much the same way.

The question, then, was, why weren't we together? Why had she ended things between us?

I repeated the question in my head that I'd cried out loud the other day. What am I not seeing, Rosa?

18

Jaicon

"Have I told you lately how annoyed I am with you for accepting Merrigan fucking 'Fatale' Shaw-Butler's offer to head up one of K19's units?" O said. "And, my God, is her name long enough now?"

"I don't think she typically includes 'fucking' when introducing herself. She probably doesn't use Fatale much anymore, either."

"I am not a fan."

I smiled. "You never have been, and that's because she terrifies you."

O made a noise that sounded like "harrumph," which I took as an admission that, yes, Fatale was probably the only person on earth Oleander feared.

"We could use you over here, by the way. Wouldn't a UN coalition fall under the heading of 'Allied Intelligence'?"

"I've already spoken with Merrigan about it."

"Oh. What prompted that conversation?"

"I'm not sure. Perhaps it was because everyone in Shere is sick of hearing you bitch about my not being there. By the way, I'm leaving for London this afternoon."

"Gatwick is closer."

Given I was born in the UK and had lived there the majority of my life, I was well aware of regional airports. "I'm stopping by the flat before coming to Shere."

"Copy that," she grumbled. "Just hurry your arse up. Poseidon is a bloody bear over this fucking auction and our inability to track the IP's origin."

The flight to London was miserable due to the storms raging over the North Atlantic Ocean. I couldn't help but draw a connection to the wrath of Poseidon.

I hadn't realized how much I missed my flat until I set foot in it. Edmund and I had purchased it for an ungodly sum shortly after we were married. With three bedrooms, it was far too large for one person, but then, it had never been intended for me to reside in alone.

One of the bedrooms had been set up as an office we shared. Another, originally slated as a nursery, remained empty. Four walls, painted a neutral color. A blank canvas, we'd said. I hadn't been there, hadn't even opened the door, since the accident, and I had no intention of doing so now. It was hard enough walking into the bedroom Edmund and I had shared. Perhaps it was time to put the flat on the market. I doubted I'd ever live in London again. While I hadn't decided where the headquarters of K19 Allied Intelligence would be, I could say it would definitively not be here.

The only things truly difficult to give up were the spectacular river views from the twentieth floor. That, I'd miss. Not that I thought about it much when I wasn't in residence.

I made myself a mental note to contact an agent about listing it, then took one more look around. Yes, listing it was the right decision. This was where *Edmund and I* had lived, and while it was too soon for me to let go of him entirely—maybe I'd never be able to—selling the flat would definitely be a step in the right direction.

"I cannot tell you how happy I am to see you. Finally, someone I don't have to explain every bloody thing to," said Oleander when we cheek-kissed.

The list of former agents and operatives who made up the five coalition task forces was beyond impressive. I'd even heard Wren Whittaker and her husband, Wilder, were consulting. Wilder was a former MI5 agent who had been in the running for chief of MI6 after Merrigan turned the position down. When Wilder declined, Z was appointed.

As for Wren, not only was she Z's daughter, she was considered to be one of the preeminent intelligent agents in the world, including all those who preceded her. I doubted she required any explanation from Oleander about anything.

"This must be Esencia," said the woman I'd just been thinking about.

"It's an honor to meet you, ma'am."

"Oh, my goodness. If I didn't hail from Texas, where women are called ma'am regardless of their age, I might be worried about how much gray is showin' through." She leaned forward. "They say you aren't supposed to color your hair when you're pregnant, but I can guarantee you my mama didn't follow those orders, and my brother and I turned out just fine."

I had no idea what to say in response, so I just stood there like a bloody carp.

"Hello, I'm Wilder," said the man who'd grown even more ridiculously handsome since we'd first met. "Wait. I know you, don't I?"

Wren elbowed her husband. "They say women get pregnancy brain, but I swear Wild's got it way worse than me."

He put his arm around her shoulders. "It's all the sleepless nights I spend watching you grow more beautiful with every passing minute."

I spun around on Oleander when I heard her groan.

"What? You just arrived. The rest of us have had to listen to this drivel for weeks."

My eyes opened wide. Had she truly just insulted the greatest spy who'd ever lived right in front of her face?

"Again, it was a pleasure to meet you, Esencia. Wilder and I will leave you and O alone since all she's been carrying on about is how much she's looking forward to your being here." Thankfully, Wren was smiling when she walked away.

"So, tell me all about Tryst Avila," O began once we were alone.

"*Tryst Avila?* Bloody hell. What have you heard and who from?"

"That would be me," said Zeppelin, and we cheek-kissed when he approached. "Welcome to Shere."

I smacked his arm. "Who would've thought you'd be a gossip?"

"Everyone," muttered Magnet. "How are you, Esencia? Good to see you." We cheek-kissed as well.

"I have to admit, it's nice to be back in the UK."

Magnet raised a brow. "I suppose, but the ranch in Mexico certainly has its charms."

"One charm in particular, so I've heard," Oleander mumbled.

"Stop it. Tryst Avila is a very nice man who has been a tremendous help by allowing us to stage the Felixstowe victims' reunification in the Mexican state of Sonora." I caught a look pass between her, Zep, and Magnet but chose to pretend I didn't. "Shall we get to work?"

"Yes, I wanted to talk to you about—"

"Nope. She's mine. I made that abundantly clear before she arrived." Oleander said to Zep before dragging me from the kitchen and into a solarium in another part of the house.

"This is lovely. It's Cayman's place, yes?"

"Yes," she said, closing the door behind her. "So, back to Tryst. Tell me everything."

Before I could scold her again, the door opened and Poseidon walked in. "I heard a rumor you'd arrived. Thanks for crossing the pond, Jacy." Like with the other men, we cheek-kissed.

"We were in the middle of something," said O, crossing her arms and tapping her foot.

Rather than leaving us to talk, Poseidon walked over to a sofa and took a seat. "Let's get to it, then."

I'd been in Shere two weeks, and we'd made no progress on figuring out where the impending auction was taking place, nor had we developed any leads of where the women shown on the site were being held.

"Bloody fucking hell!" I heard Poseidon shout from another room.

"Now what?" Oleander muttered.

I followed her to find out.

"The site has been taken down," he said when we entered the room, "and sixteen million pounds moved in, then out of the AMPS account in the last twenty-four hours."

"We've been monitoring the site. The auction was still delayed," said O.

"They must've set up an alternate site," I suggested.

Poseidon got up and stormed out of the room. Oleander followed.

19

Jaicon

Eight months later

While we'd continued to monitor the dark web, months had gone by with little to no activity on the AMPS investigation. Our working theory was the human traffickers responsible for the sex-slave auctions were intentionally lying low.

Each of the five task forces had other inquiries running concurrently. The US and UK teams were focusing the majority of our efforts on the ten shipping containers that arrived in the port of Felixstowe.

We were divided into smaller teams. One was focused on who'd abducted the victims in the first place and whether it was one trafficking organization or multiple. Since I'd interviewed most of the victims, I was assigned to this one.

A second's mandate was determining who owned the ten containers. As anticipated, all ten were registered to shell corps.

A third group dove deeper into the intended destinations of the ten containers. The initial investigation into this hadn't gone anywhere. Like the containers themselves, the abandoned warehouses and industrial parks shown on the manifests were also owned by shell corps.

If there was a connection between those shell corps and AMPS, it would give us a lot to go on.

"What if there was more than one trafficking ring with containers on that ship?" I said to O when we took a short break and went outside. I wasn't working with that particular team, but it seemed worth looking into. Meaning, if we found the true owner of one, it wouldn't necessarily imply they owned them all.

"We're working that angle."

Oleander didn't seem herself. Maybe the world of play-by-the-rules intelligence was getting to her.

"What's going on with you? Need to assassinate some evil-doer?"

At least, that got a smile out of her. "Assassination, yes. Evil-doer, not necessarily."

I raised a brow.

"Poseidon."

"I see. Not playing nicely in the sandbox?" I asked.

"It isn't that, but he doesn't believe we should focus so much of our efforts on searching for Pharaoh. He believes once the other questions are answered, we'll have what we need to find her. I believe once we find her, our questions will be answered."

"Couldn't you approach it from opposite directions and hope to meet in the middle?"

She shook her head. "With a reasonable person."

"You don't work for him, O. Go above his head."

In a very unlike-Oleander move, she shrugged her shoulder. "What about you?"

"Me? How am I involved?"

"Not what I'm referring to." She leveled her gaze at me.

"Sorry, O. I've no idea what you're talking about."

"You've turned into a robot. It's all about the mission and nothing else. Do you think no one notices you up at zero three hundred, toiling away while the rest of us are smart enough to rest?"

"Two things, my friend. First, you're overstepping. Second, you have a lot of nerve, calling me out on something you have done throughout your entire career."

She sat on the grass and motioned for me to do the same. "Are you under the impression I don't know what's really going on here? I have done precisely what you're doing for most of my career. That means I get it, Jaicon. I know you're keeping busy so you can avoid looking at what's not working in the rest of your life."

"And here I thought I left the zen master in Mexico," I muttered. "Go ahead and enlighten me, wise one."

She smirked. "The zen master, eh?"

"Of course that's what you'd pick up on."

"He's the reason you're a robot."

I got to my feet. "I've had enough, Oleander. Don't attempt to manufacture another mystery since what you're working on isn't going well."

She grabbed my wrist. "It's four years this week."

"Do you think I'm unaware of how long my husband's been gone?" Oleander didn't know about the baby I'd lost, and I had no intention of telling her, or anyone else, for that matter.

"Zeppelin said you lit up when you were around Tryst."

"Zeppelin can sod off. You as well." I tried to shake free from her grasp, but she wouldn't let go.

"Jacy, it's been four bloody years. You're thirty-two years old—"

"Thirty-three."

"Thank you for making my argument stronger. You're three and thirty and have spent the last eight months throwing yourself so deeply into work there's no room for anyone or anything else."

"*Again,* you do the same thing, O."

"We aren't talking about me."

This time, I wrenched my arm away hard enough for her to let go. "We aren't talking about me, either."

"Do you honestly believe Edmund would approve of what you're doing with your life?" she shouted after me.

"Edmund is dead," I hollered back.

She ran around in front of me. "Precisely my point. He is dead. You are not. Although you might as well be."

"Fuck off, O."

She grabbed my arms. "Maybe I would if I didn't care about you as much as I do. But it's too late for that. You're my best mate, and I hate to see you so miserable."

"What would you have me do?"

"Go back to Mexico."

"This from the woman who begged me to come to Shere?"

"You aren't as much help as I thought you'd be."

"I have no reason to return. Plus, that ship has sailed, as they say."

"I'll give you a reason. You will be far more effective at looking for traffickers out of Mexico if you're actually in Mexico."

"I told him it would never work between us. He's moved on."

She shook her head. "He hasn't."

I put my hands on my hips. "Oh, really? And you've had a conversation with the man?"

"I have not, but someone else who cares about you has."

"Bloody hell. I made Merrigan promise not to interfere."

"Actually, you made her promise not to push you into something you weren't ready for."

I raised a brow. "I thought you hated the woman. Now, you're bosom buddies?"

"United by our concern for you."

"Tell me how you see this playing out. I travel to Mexico, knock on his door, and say I heard he wasn't over me?"

"You'll figure out what to do when you get there."

"I'm not going."

Oleander shook her head. "Yes. You are. Would you like to know why I'm so certain?"

"If I said no—"

"Because you've already decided to go."

"I haven't."

O rolled her eyes. "Go look in the mirror and say you aren't going to Mexico. See if it's as easy to lie to yourself as it is to me."

"I have responsibilities here in England." I'd listed my flat six months ago and hadn't had a single offer.

"I have to admit I was as surprised as Merrigan that you didn't return at least for a few days after the fire."

My eyes scrunched. "What fire?"

O was a master at hiding her reactions to nearly everything. So the fact her mouth was hanging open meant she was truly stunned.

"Oleander, *what fire?*"

"Tryst's meditation center burned to the ground."

I was so angry no one had mentioned it to me. I was shaking. "How long have you known?"

"Not long, maybe a week. It happened months ago, though."

"Excuse me."

I didn't bloody well care what time it was in California; I pulled out my mobile and rang Merrigan.

"What's this about a fire?"

"Hello, Jaicon."

"Don't fucking toy with me. Why wasn't I informed?"

"I honestly thought you knew."

"Knew? If I'd known, I would've caught the next flight out of London. He must be devastated."

"He was. I'm not sure if he still is."

Clearly, Merrigan didn't know Tryst as well as she thought she did. That meditation center was everything to him. That and the equine program. If she thought he'd get over it with nary a care, she knew nothing about the man.

"I'm leaving for Mexico as soon as I can get a flight."

"Would you like Doc to make arrangements?"

"If you mean for a flight, then no. I don't want to wait that long. I'll be in touch."

I turned around and saw O right behind me. Based on her smile, she'd heard every word.

I was on my way to the airport when I received an alert on my mobile. An offer came in this morning on my flat. The buyer was willing to pay the full price.

20

Tryst

When I saw the alert that Jaicon had entered through the ranch gate, it was all I could do not to run out of the barn, jump in my truck, and drive in her direction.

I had no idea why she was here, and I didn't care. Just to be able to look into her eyes would be enough for me. I was still trying to figure out whether to get in my truck or wait, when she pulled up.

She got out and rushed over to me. "I heard about the meditation center. My God, I'm so sorry."

When she walked straight into my arms, I closed my eyes and breathed in her scent. I focused on every place our bodies touched, trying to commit exactly how it felt to memory. When she rested her head on my chest, I raised one hand and stroked her hair.

"I missed you so," I whispered, hoping my blunt statement wouldn't make her uncomfortable and result in her stepping back.

Warmth spread throughout my body when she said, "I missed you too."

"Jaicon." Her name was like a prayer on my lips. I so wanted to kiss her. Did I dare? No. I couldn't. First, I needed to know why she was here. However, rather than both of us tiptoeing around our feelings, I decided to be forthright with mine. "It feels so good to hold you." When she tried pulling away, I used my arm to hold her close to me. "Why have you come?" I asked.

"I didn't learn of the fire until forty-eight hours ago. I apologize for not getting here sooner."

I cupped her cheek, looked into her eyes, and smiled. "The fire has been out for quite some time, my love."

"I was worried about you. What happened? How did it start?"

"It was a terrible accident."

"I know how much the center meant to you."

I caressed her cheek with my thumb. "It still does."

"Tryst, I'm sorry. Before I left, I said—"

I put my fingertip on her lips. "I don't care what you said before. I only want to hear what you're saying now."

At the sound of a horse neighing, we both turned our heads and looked. Cariño stood near the fence rail. Her nostrils were soft and round, and her tail swished back and forth. "She missed you as much as I did," I said, bringing her hand to my lips and kissing the back of it. "The center has been rebuilt. Would you like to see it?"

Her eyes were wide open. "Of course. Forgive me, but I'm stunned. I thought it was a total loss."

"It was. Within a matter of minutes, all that was left was the scorched earth. Would you like to go now, or would you rather say hello to Cariño first?"

Jaicon smiled, and the same warmth I'd felt earlier spread throughout my body.

"I imagine her feelings would be quite hurt if I didn't stop and say hello."

"She would be devastated."

"Hey, Tryst. I didn't know Jacy was comin' back," said Tex, approaching me as I watched her interact with the horse.

"Neither did I."

"Pleasant surprise, then?"

"The best."

Tex rubbed my shoulder. "I'm happy for you, Tryst. Let me know if there's anything I can do."

"Many thanks." Tex was about to walk away, but I called him back.

"There is one thing, but you'll need help from some of the others."

"Anything. Just name it, boss."

We walked a few steps farther away from the corral. "These are the GPS coordinates," I said after explaining what I wanted him to do.

"I'll get right on it as soon as they're done." He motioned with his head to the corral.

"They're done." I smiled and called out to Jacy. "Ready?"

She kissed the horse's nose, then came bounding over to me.

"I'm anxious for you to see the amazing work that's been done," I said, taking her hand.

"I'm so intrigued." When we rounded a bend and the meditation center was in view, she gasped. "How?"

"I have many friends who showed up to help."

"*Caballeros*, by any chance?" She winked.

"Maybe."

When we approached the entrance, I asked her to close her eyes, then led her inside. "Okay, open."

She put her hands on her cheeks, and her eyes filled with tears. "Tryst, I'm speechless. It's so beautiful. The floors are gorgeous."

I walked over to the wall switch and flipped it. "Come." We both toed off our shoes, and I led her to the center of the space.

"Heat!" she said several seconds later. "How brilliant!"

"George will appreciate the compliment."

Her eyes scrunched.

"He is an architect and a dear friend of mine."

"What's over there?" she asked, pointing.

"Those are *puja*—sacred rooms."

She nodded and turned toward the windows.

"Jaicon?"

"Yes?"

"Would you like to see one?"

She studied me. "Only if you want to show me."

I took her hand and led her to Rosa's room. I unlocked the door and motioned for her to enter. My heart nearly burst with joy when the first thing she did was ring the bells. Next, she stepped to her left and, walking clockwise, approached the *mandir* and bowed to the lone *mūrti*. "Namaste." She turned to me. "This is for Rosa, isn't it?"

I bowed my head. "It is."

She motioned to the *mandir*. "Did you build this?"

I smiled and nodded.

"It's truly beautiful and such a lovely tribute."

"You're the first person to see it other than me," I confessed.

"I'm honored."

I told her about my intention to place Saraswati and how the *mūrti* broke apart in my hand. Jaicon didn't comment right away but appeared to be deep in thought.

"I wondered why there was just the one."

"I have not been able to decide on another."

She nodded. "The answer will come to you."

"What would you like to do now?" I asked when I led her outside.

"Are you, by chance, hungry? I haven't eaten since, um, yesterday, maybe?"

I pulled her close to me and kissed her temple. "I am famished."

"Can we please go to Cenaduria Dona Maria? I've been craving her chile relleno."

I took her to the restaurant that had room for only ten patrons. Since we were the only two there at the time, we did not rush. Over margaritas, appetizers, and finally chile relleno, which we shared, Jaicon filled me in on what she'd been doing the last few months.

"I have this feeling Manual Varilla and AMPS are connected," she said, leaning in closer to me. "I just haven't been able to connect them."

"My nephews Salazar and Rascon came to help rebuild the center right after the fire. They mentioned something about working with you."

Jaicon took a bite of the relleno and closed her eyes. This is *so* good. It's a tossup between this"—she pointed to her plate with her fork—"and curry. I ate so much of it while I was in the UK, but I'll never tire of it."

"One of my favorite spots for curry is right here in Alamos. It's Papel Dosa."

She grinned at me. "Holding out on me, Tryst? Why am I just hearing about this now?"

"There are many, many things around here I haven't shown you yet." One in particular, although I doubted I'd be able to tonight.

"I'm looking forward to all of it," I said, smiling.

"Seriously, the relleno is so good. You don't mind if I finish it, do you?"

I grabbed her hand that held the fork and brought it to my mouth. "Mmm," I groaned, closing my eyes and savoring the flavors of the poblano chile peppers stuffed with queso asadero. "You're right. It is my favorite relleno too." When I opened my eyes, the expression on Jaicon's face had changed. Rather than the violet blue her eyes were mere moments ago, her black pupils were now ringed with a thin line of color. I vividly remembered the last time I noticed desire in her eyes. It was her first day on the ranch, and even then, I wanted her more than my next breath.

She cleared her throat. "So, um, what have you been doing with yourself?"

"I have a project that has taken much of my time."

"I'd love to hear about it."

"Not yet, but soon. I promise." I cupped the back of her neck with my palm and drew her closer, brushing her lips with mine.

When my cell phone vibrated with a tone I used specifically for messages from the barns, I broke our kiss. "My apologies. I need to make sure there is no emergency."

While I read the message, she took a long drink of water.

Everything is ready for you, boss, the message read. I smiled.

"Good news rather than an emergency?" she asked, fanning her face.

"Were the chiles too hot?"

"No." Since she didn't elaborate, I didn't pry.

"Are you finished, or would you like to order something else?" I asked.

"I'm finished."

"There's something else I want to show you."

"Does it have to do with the project that's taken much of your time?"

"Perhaps." I tossed several bills on the table, hollered out to Dona Maria that we were leaving, and grabbed Jaicon's hand. "Come," I said, pulling her behind me.

The drive from the restaurant took twenty minutes. Once we reached the ranch's main gates, I kept driving until we came to another that required I open it by hand. My earlier request had been for the brush to be cut back on the dirt road so I could navigate it in my truck.

I drove through, then exited the vehicle a second time to close the gate behind us. I anticipated Jaicon asking where we were going, but she didn't. I glanced over at her and down at her hand, which was tucked under her leg.

She followed my gaze. "Sorry. I've always done it when I'm excited. You know, like Christmas morning."

Rather than put the truck in gear, I reached over and pulled her close enough to kiss. "If I didn't have to drive, I would probably sit on my hands with excitement too."

"Don't poke fun."

"Believe me. I am not." I put the truck in gear. "Hold on tight, my love. This will be a very bumpy ride."

I glanced over at her a few seconds later, wondering if my use of the endearment upset her, but she didn't appear to have noticed.

A few minutes later, we crested a rise in the road and our destination came into view. The house I pulled in front of looked as though it belonged more in Jaipur, India, than it did on a ranch in Mexico. However, every time I drove out here, I was struck by its beauty.

"Where are we?" Jaicon asked.

I cocked my head, laughed, and shrugged.

"What?"

"I realized I don't know how to describe it."

"Okay. Well. It's a house. A very beautiful house."

I nodded slowly. "Thank you."

"It's your house, then, yes?"

"In a manner of speaking."

When Jaicon got out of the truck, I did too. She met me halfway and put her hands on my shoulders. "Tryst, is this *your* house?"

"Yes."

"Do you live here?"

"No."

Her eyes scrunched. "Have you ever lived in it?"

"I have not."

She nodded. "Would you like to show it to me?"

"Very much so." I led her up the side steps of the wraparound veranda and was on my way to the front door when she put her hand on my arm.

"Wait. Tell me about the outside first." She pointed to a sitting area in the center section near the front door, then to the view.

I took her hand and led her to the teak benches I'd built and affixed directly to the veranda's support columns. She ran her hand over the carved wood. "This is beautiful. Are you the artisan?"

"I am."

"Again, exquisite." She sat down, facing away from the door. "North?" she asked, pointing in front of her.

"Yes."

"Auspicious," she said with a nod of her head. She looked over at the parked truck, then at the dirt road. "The gate faces north as well, yes?"

I smiled. "It does."

Jaicon stood, clasped her hands behind her, walked to the door, and waited. When I opened it, she removed her shoes before stepping inside.

"The design is traditional *naalukettu*, meaning a quadrangular structure built around a courtyard or open space."

"May I?" she asked.

"Of course."

I followed her into the foyer, separated from the great room by a two-sided fireplace. She walked to the right; I went left.

"This would be a sitting area." I motioned to the empty space.

Jaicon spun in a circle and looked up. "The vaulted ceilings are lovely." She continued to the right, through an archway. "Kitchen and…"

"Dining room."

"Ah. Makes sense. And on the opposite side?"

"A sitting room in front. Behind it, an office."

I watched her enter each room, spin in a circle, then go on to the next.

"A bedroom to your left."

Jaicon stuck her head in the door but did not enter the room.

"A bathroom and another bedroom?" She pointed.

"Yes."

"What is this room?" she asked when she reached the rear of the house.

"It could be used for meditation." I walked inside, and she followed. "Or a guest suite since it has a full bath."

She turned in the opposite direction and walked to the other side of the house. "A covered arbor?" she commented as she passed through.

I nodded.

"Lovely," she murmured before stepping into my favorite room of the house.

I'd envisioned the master suite to be a sanctuary. It had enough room for an oversized king bed and a sitting area with another double-sided fireplace that opened to another private place to relax on the veranda.

There were two walk-in closets and a luxurious bathing area with a jetted tub designed for two people to enjoy, along with a rectangular-shaped shower with fixtures on either end and a private toilet area.

She stepped out of the room, passing the laundry area and another bathroom on her way back to the kitchen. There, she ran her hand over the leathered granite counters.

"It's as large as the master suite," she said, again spinning in a circle.

"Two of the most important rooms."

"Wow, Tryst. This is a dream house."

I walked over to the courtyard and looked up at the glass ceiling and pointed. "Not a dream to clean."

She laughed. "It would be a labor of love, though, wouldn't it? Then again, it all was, wasn't it?"

"Yes," I whispered.

"Where is your furniture?"

"I haven't gotten that far."

"What a shame."

"Why do you say it that way?"

"I would've dearly loved to sleep here tonight."

"Perhaps you still can."

"Perhaps *I* can?"

21

Jaicon

I held my breath, waiting for Tryst's response. There were a thousand questions I wanted to ask, starting with, "Did you build this for your wife?" but now, I wondered if I'd gone too far with my implication that I wanted to sleep here with him.

"Jaicon?"

"Right. Sorry. Overstepped. We should probably get back now."

Rather than walk toward the door, Tryst approached me, crowding me against the wall and pinning me with an arm on either side of me. "I want nothing more than to make love to you. Here. Tonight. Now, in fact. But first, we must talk."

I tried to dip under his arm, but he caught me, so I rested my forehead on his chest. "Talk."

He used one finger on my chin to raise my face so I was looking at him. "Tell me why you returned to Mexico."

"Merrigan told me about the fire."

He shook his head.

"What do you mean, no?"

"That is not why you came."

"I was concerned about you."

He shook his head again.

"Why do you keep doing that? Do you think you know my mind better than I do?"

"I know when you're not being truthful."

"How nice. You're accusing me of lying to you?"

He leaned forward and rested his cheek against mine. "Why are you here, Jaicon?"

"I couldn't…" My eyes filled with tears. "I don't know. I told myself I wasn't ready. I'm not ready. I just…I couldn't stay away."

He let out the breath I hadn't realized he was holding. "I am so glad you're here."

"I have to ask. Whose house is this, Tryst? Is it Rosa's house? Did you build it for your late wife?"

He shook his head again. Slowly.

"Who then?"

"I have asked myself that question many times."

"Did you ever answer?"

"I don't think I knew before."

"Tryst…"

"After the fire and the reconstruction of the meditation center was complete, I felt purposeless. That's why I built it."

"Do you intend to live in it?" I asked.

"I think I would like to."

"You'll need furniture."

He laughed, and I smiled, but his eyes scrunched. "Do you have any idea how much I want to kiss you?"

"What are you waiting for?"

His tongue swept the line of my lips, coaxing them open. Then it slipped inside, to swirl against mine. He pulled away, nipping my lip before soothing it, and trailed more kisses from my mouth to my jaw, then up my cheek, to my ear.

"Jacy." My name sounded like a sigh, and he stunned me by stepping away from me. "What happened that made you leave Mexico?"

"Is there somewhere we can sit?"

He led me out the front door and to the built-in sitting area. "Will you be warm enough?"

"If you sit beside me, I think so."

Once we'd both settled onto the bench, he draped his arm behind me.

I took a deep breath and let it out slowly. There was so much I wanted to say, and while I'd rehearsed it over and over again, I found myself struggling with where to begin.

"We were at Butler Ranch. It was when Los Caballeros had an emergency meeting."

"I remember that evening. You slept in my arms the night before."

"Earlier in the day, you and I talked about children, and you told me how looking into fertility issues was how you discovered Rosa was sick."

He nodded.

"You asked me if my husband and I ever talked about having a family. I told you we hadn't." I took another deep breath. "I wasn't honest with you."

He studied me, but I saw no judgment in his eyes, only that he was paying attention.

"It wasn't that we talked about it per se. More… God, this is really hard."

"Take your time."

"We were out for dinner the night of the accident, and I told him I was pregnant."

Tryst nodded in the slow, wise way he often did.

"Later that night, I lost the baby."

When his eyes closed, I could feel the pain he experienced on my behalf. "I'm so sorry, Jacy."

"We hadn't talked about it. We hadn't planned to get pregnant. It just happened."

"I understand."

"I don't know if I can have more children. I never asked."

Tryst pulled me closer to him. "Thank you for telling me these things about your life. I am honored that you trust me to do so."

"I dozed off while you were at the meeting and was awoken by a dream. I have nightmares about the accident all the time, but this was different. Edmund, my husband, looked much like he had at dinner. The difference was he was holding a little girl. Right before I jarred myself awake, she reached out for me. She called me Mama."

"What pain you must've been in."

"I'm sorry I didn't tell you."

Tryst shook his head. "You were not ready to share that part of your life with me. I understand."

"You asked why I came, and I told you it was because of the fire. It's true, but it was also just an excuse to see you. I wanted to see you. I want to see you, Tryst. Am I too late?"

He looked as though he was in pain, making me want to take back every word I'd said and catch the next flight to the UK.

"I have dreamed of the day you returned to the ranch. To me."

"You haven't answered me, Tryst. Am I too late?"

He kissed both my eyelids, then each cheek, then my lips. "You could never be too late."

I waved my hand in the direction of the front door of the house. "What about this? Is there someone else in your life, Tryst? Someone you built this for?"

He shook his head. "I told you before I didn't know why I was building it. Only that I had to." He cupped my cheek again. "There is no one else, Jaicon. Only you." When he leaned forward to kiss me again, I felt scorched, branded, as though he'd just claimed me as his. "It is all I can do not to…" He sighed and looked up at the night sky. "The first time you and I make love, I want it to be in this house. In a bed we share. Your naked body illuminated by the fire's glow."

I shuddered, and my eyes drooped. "I want that too, but I think we need a bed."

He laughed out loud. "We need a lot of things, but mostly a bed." His expression changed, and he stared into my eyes. "I do not want to rush this, Jacy. I want us both to be certain it is right. That we're ready."

"I understand. I know I just told you I want the same thing you do, but I also want to take things slow. I want to be certain. I don't want to hurt you again."

He pinched the skin on his wrist and grimaced.

"Why did you do that?"

"I wanted to be sure I wasn't dreaming again."

"Again?" I asked.

He nodded. "Almost every night. Now, I know it's why I built this house. I dreamed of us being here. Each time, I woke alone…"

"I'm sorry, Tryst. I'm so sorry I hurt you."

"When you said things went the way they were supposed to, that neither of us was ready for a romantic relationship, it felt like a knife to my heart."

"I'm—"

He pressed his lips to mine. "I have more I need to say."

I nodded.

"I broke down your words so many times. They replayed in my head over and over again until, one day,

I finally heard the part that really mattered. I heard that neither of us was ready. I *wanted* to be. But you were right. There were—are—things I haven't resolved in my mind or my heart."

"Oh. Um. I see."

He smiled and kissed the tip of my nose. "You do not."

"Then, help me to, Tryst."

"I believe we both have things to resolve, but we do not have to be apart to do so. We can help each other."

"Do you really think so?"

"I do."

I leaned forward, burying my head in the crook of his neck. "I'm frightened."

"As am I. But we will help each other overcome our fears."

"I suppose we should return to the *casita* now."

He shook his head.

"No?"

"I cannot be apart from you."

"Nor I, you."

"What do we do?" I asked.

"Improvise."

22

Tryst

"Wait here," I said before going out to the trailer I'd used as an office and for storage when I was heavy into the house's construction. I'd kept pillows, sleeping bags, and even a queen-size air mattress for the nights I was too tired to return to the other house. Thankfully, I'd bought it all new and only used it a time or two.

Jaicon's face lit up when I came inside and dropped the pile on the floor, by the fireplace.

"One more thing." I ran back out to grab a few logs.

When I returned, she already had the air mattress partially blown up. I lit the fire first, then helped assemble the "bed."

"It's not the fanciest of accommodations…" I said, opening one sleeping bag all the way to place under us, then the other for over.

Jaicon smiled. "It's magical."

"I thought of one more thing."

"What else could we possibly need?" She winked.

"Water."

"Right. You best hurry, though. This is so cozy I may already be asleep by the time you return."

I set the bottles of water I'd fetched on either side of the mattress, then crawled under the sleeping bag when Jaicon held it up for me.

She turned her back to my front, and I wrapped an arm around her waist.

"This is another thing I dreamed of."

"Me too," she said, trailing her fingers over my hand and arm.

I snuggled her close, loving the feel of her body against mine. It didn't matter that we were fully clothed.

"What are you thinking about?" she asked.

"How good you feel in my arms. How happy I am you're here. How I'm still afraid I'll wake up and this will all have been a dream." I nuzzled her neck, breathing in her wondrous scent. "What are you thinking?"

"We should make curry for dinner tomorrow night."

Her response was so unexpected, I laughed. "Yeah?"

"How well-equipped is your kitchen?"

"Not at all, I fear."

She shrugged. "We'll shop tomorrow. Maybe we can even pick out a bed."

I turned her in my arms so I could see her face. Rather than speak, I stared into her eyes. After a moment, I said, "Jaicon?" I wanted to ask if she planned to remain in Mexico. I wanted to know for how long, but I couldn't figure out how.

"Ask me."

I shook my head. "It's…I'm…rarely at such a loss for words."

She smiled and raised her hand to cup my cheek. "The moment I crossed the threshold, I felt as though this is where I belong. I know it seems fast, and I know I've given you mixed signals in the past, but being here, on your ranch, gives me a sense of peace like none I've ever known. Even when I fought against it, my subconscious wanted to be here. I *longed* to be here. To be with you." She leaned forward and kissed me. "One of the other operatives, Oleander, said I'd consumed myself with work in order to avoid dealing with the rest of my life. I can't say it was limited to one specific conversation, but something compelled me to get on a plane. Maybe her words served as the final puzzle piece that made it all fit together."

"*Your* words fill me—my heart—with so much joy."

"Being here with you, in your arms, does the same for me." She closed her eyes, shook her head, and smiled. "I listed my flat in London, and for months, no one even looked at it. I was on my way to the airport when I received an email saying someone wanted to buy it and would pay the full price. It may sound crazy, but I saw it as a sign. London was no longer my home, but I didn't feel homeless. I got on the plane, knowing it would take me to the place I was supposed to be. Supposed to spend my life." She chuckled. "If those words scare you, just know they terrify me."

"They thrill and excite me. They make me so happy I could burst. I feel no fear. I built this house for you, Jaicon. I know that now. The only memories it will hold are ones of you and me, of our life together."

She wiggled. "Tryst?"

"Yes, my love."

"We really need to get a bed."

It was an-hour-and-a-half drive to Ciudad Obregón, a city ten times the size of Alamos, where there were stores carrying what we'd need. We spent the morning selecting pieces of furniture—including a bed frame and mattress set—that would be delivered and set up before the end of the day.

"Are there any pieces you want to have brought from your other house?" Jaicon asked between stores.

There weren't. Like the house itself, what we filled it with would be ours alone.

We packed the truck with as many pots, pans, dishes, and linens as it would hold. While we were gone, I'd asked Maria, the head of the ranch's housekeeping staff, to fill the pantry and refrigerator with the same staples she would've for any guest on my property. Finally, on the return trip to Alamos, we stopped at a market to pick up the ingredients for curry.

Throughout the day, one of us would stop the other to embrace, kiss, or just to stare into each other's eyes.

We were driving out of the city on our way to Alamos when Jaicon spotted a place I'd visited several times since I made Mexico my home full time.

"Is that a temple?" she asked.

"It is. Would you like to stop?"

"I feel as though we're supposed to. Do I sound like I've gone off the rails?"

"You know the importance of listening to your intuition as much as, or more than, anyone else." I pulled onto the road leading to the sacred place and parked.

"There's a store?" she asked, pointing to a sign that read, "Tienda de Regalos."

"One I have visited many times." The shop carried *mūrtis* of varying sizes and was where I'd purchased them for both the temple and the meditation center.

I watched Jaicon peruse the shelves, studying the description of each of the sculptures.

"I would like to purchase that one," I said, pointing.

Jaicon read the description out loud. "Ganga represents the eternal power of Brahman that gives life, nourishes life, purifies life, facilitates renewal and rebirth, and liberates life." She looked up at me. "Ganga is the goddess of forgiveness."

I nodded. "There is another over here. Tell me what you think." She followed me to a set of shelves. "The elephant-headed Ganesha is the lord of beginnings and the remover of obstacles."

"I'm not sure what to say," she whispered.

I leaned in closer. "Have I upset you?"

Jaicon shook her head. "I just feel like I shouldn't have a say in what you place in your wife's sacred room. If that's what these are for."

I raked my beard with my fingers. "When you asked me if the room was to honor Rosa, do you remember my response?"

"I'm sorry. I do not."

"I said 'in part.' What I meant is the sacred room is to honor the Goddess Mahadevi. She is the supreme deity and combination of all the goddesses." I led her to where the goddess's sculptures and paintings were displayed. "Some consider her the spiritual mother of all. She forgives our mistakes so our lives can blossom like the lotus flower she holds."

"That is a beautiful tribute, Tryst."

I leaned forward and kissed her cheek. I wouldn't say it now because I sensed it would make her uncomfortable, but the sacred room in the meditation center honored her too. It honored all women.

Rosa was the first I'd loved as a man loves a woman. For many years, I believed she would be the only. Then the gods and goddesses brought Jaicon into my life and me into hers.

A feeling of peace washed over me. I'd never experienced this phenomenon outside of a temple, but at that moment, I had total clarity, and Jaicon was the reason.

We belonged together. We belonged to each other. She was mine, and I was hers. We were standing in a temple's gift shop, surrounded by deities, and all I could think about was joining our bodies together, becoming one as we were intended to be.

I leaned forward again and kissed the soft flesh beneath her ear. "Jaicon, let's go home," I whispered.

Her eyes drooped, and her right hand clung to my arm. Desire had overwhelmed her like it had me. The power of it could not be denied. "Please, Tryst."

Our purchases could wait for another day. Loving Jaicon could not.

I was in a daze, driving to *El Lugar de Curación*. It felt as though the truck represented a cocoon that Jaicon and I would soon emerge from. Life was about to change for both of us. As soon as we set foot in the house, I now knew without any doubt or hesitation I'd built for us. Jaicon and me. Had she never returned to my life, it would've sat empty. But then, I knew she would, and when she did, I had to be ready. I worked tirelessly to create a dwelling that was hers and mine alone. A place where we could make love without the ghosts of the past surrounding us.

I reached over, took her hand, brought it to my lips, and kissed her palm.

"Tryst, I…" Her pupils were black with a thin blue line ringing them. Recognizing the level of her desire made me even harder.

"I feel the same, my love."

"I want you so badly I can't think about anything else." I'd never heard Jaicon whine, but the want I heard excited me even more.

"Not much longer. When we arrive home, we will go inside, and I will remove your clothes, and you will do the same for me."

"Yes." Her eyes drifted closed, and she shuddered.

I'd requested Tex bring some of the ranch hands to the house earlier when I received an alert the furniture was to be delivered. I prayed, that when we arrived, they would be gone.

I drove up to the gate that would soon be replaced with another similar to what was at the ranch's main entrance. Jumping out of the truck, opened it, then got back in. Rather than stopping to close it, I kept going. When we rounded the bend of the dirt road, I breathed a sigh of relief that there were no vehicles parked near the house.

Pulling up, I cut the engine, got out, and hurried around to open Jaicon's door. When she turned, I placed my hands on her waist, and she slid down the length of my body. I kissed her then, unable to wait another moment to feel her mouth open to mine, to taste her sweetness. Every part of me longed to touch her, to make her body sing with pleasure.

She broke our kiss, took my hand, and led me to the front door. Rather than open it, I turned to face her, taking both her hands in mine.

"When we cross this threshold, we will be walking into our new life in the same way a butterfly emerges from its cocoon. Together, we will spread our wings and fly, my beloved Jacy. Before we do, there is something I must say to you." I took a deep breath and let it out slowly before saying the words I never thought I'd utter again in my life, but feeling their meaning so profoundly, I had to speak them. "I love you, Jaicon."

Her eyes filled with tears, but not in sadness. The smile that warmed me from the first time I met her, spread across her face. "I love you, Tryst."

I released one of her hands, opened the door, then gathered her in my arms, picked her up, and carried her inside. I turned, and she kicked the door closed. Rather than set her on her feet, I toed off my shoes and brought her through the house to the bedroom. Everything was as I'd asked it to be. The bed was set up in the place I'd intended it to go, and it had been made.

Setting Jaicon on its edge, I spread her legs, then dropped to my knees. I reached up and unfastened the buttons on her shirt, pulled it open, then leaned forward to press a kiss on the swell of her chest. I waited while she removed it from her arms, then reached around and released the clasp of her bra.

Seeing her perfect breasts for the first time, I had to taste the stiff pink nipples. Lowering my head, I took one into my mouth, sucking it at the same time as I gently pinched the other's tip with my fingers. When I replaced my hand with my mouth, I unfastened the button on her jeans.

As much as I wanted to take my time, I couldn't. I released the nipple with a pop, stood, and pulled her to her feet. Her soft moans urged me to hurry, and I dropped to my knees a second time. Jaicon toed off her shoes while I lowered her pants. When she stepped from them, her panties were the only barrier remaining. I used my fingers to pull them over her hips and down her thighs until they fell to the floor.

I guided her legs apart, kissing from her hip bone to her glistening pussy. She weaved her fingers in my hair, her nails raking my scalp. I spread the folds of her pussy, leaned forward, and licked the sensitive bundle of nerves. Her fingers pulled at my hair as my tongue continued to play over her.

"Sit on the bed for me," I groaned when my balls tightened, my body reminding me I did not have the control to linger. She sat on the edge and watched as I reached around and pulled my shirt over my head with one hand while she unfastened my jeans like I had hers. She pushed them and my boxers over my hips, and my steel-hard cock sprung in its release.

Her eyes roamed the length of me, then she leaned forward and licked the tip of my cock, swirling it with her tongue.

"I cannot wait, my love."

Jaicon scooted up so she rested on the pillows. Before I could demand she do so, she spread her legs. I took in every inch of her with my eyes, like she had with me. "Jacy, I want to feel your wetness, your heat, your body against mine with no barriers. If you do not want that, I will sheath myself."

"I want to feel you too," she said, struggling to speak as she writhed in anticipation.

My control slipped with her words as I pressed my cock against her slick entrance, easing into her. Jaicon arched against me.

"You are mine, and I am yours," I said, thrusting deep, then waiting until her pussy adjusted to my size. With a growl in my throat, I pulled almost all the way out, then sank back into her—hard, fast, and deep.

I felt her reach around and grasp the cheeks of my butt, deepening the connection of our bodies, then holding me still.

"Tryst," she cried out as I felt her come on my cock at the same time my own pleasure released in a torrent so powerful I shook from it.

23

Jaicon

Our days became a continuing cycle of making love, preparing food—both of us naked in the kitchen—eating, then making love again, and sleeping when we felt like it.

There was never a time in my life I felt so at peace. Tryst was everything—so handsome he took my breath away. His chiseled body excited me to the point where I found it hard to breathe as I begged him to take me again and again.

Setting up the rooms of the house had been such a joy. I'd never experienced anything like it. Until now, everywhere I'd lived had been furnished, including the flat in London, except for the one room.

Thinking about it didn't bring me the same pain it used to. I'd moved on from that time of my life with forgiveness and acceptance, thanks to Tryst.

We'd returned to the temple near Ciudad Obregón and purchased the two *mūrtis* we'd previously picked out, plus more for the meditation room we'd created in the house.

Tryst also taught me about Vastu shastra, the traditional Indian architecture based on ancient texts. I'd known some, like which direction would be the most auspicious for the house to face, but he explained more about how everything—design, layout, measurements, spatial geometrics, and arrangement—all worked together to create harmony.

He smiled when I told him I believed he was the one responsible for the harmonious life we'd settled into.

While the missions I'd worked in the UK, as well as the trafficking victims who were suffering at the hands of their captors, were always in the back of my mind, I couldn't help but appreciate every moment I spent in the house we'd made ours.

I tried not to compare Tryst and my late husband, but the truth was, I was happier here with him than I ever remembered being with Edmund.

Life, love, and day-to-day existence were so easy with Tryst. While we didn't always agree, our discussions about our differences of opinion were just that. We talked things through, then compromised. Honestly, I never dreamed life could be this good.

"Good afternoon, my love," said Tryst when he returned from the riding center. Most days, I went with him, but I stayed behind today to prepare a surprise for him. I only hoped I could do Dona Maria's secret recipe for chile relleno justice after she'd so graciously shared it with me.

He took a deep breath after we kissed. "It smells fabulous in here. What are you making?"

"A surprise, but it should be done in about an hour."

"Does that mean we have time for a quick shower?" he asked, winking.

Given we almost always showered together, which meant we also ended up making love, an hour would be quick. We never rushed when we were in each other's arms. We took our time, learning each other's bodies and what brought us the most pleasure. Like life, I never dreamed sex could be as amazing as what Tryst and I shared. "I planned it so we could, my love," I said. We shared terms of endearment freely with each other because that was what he was to me and vice versa.

Tryst and I had just finished eating the best chile relleno he'd ever had, as he'd qualified it even after I shared it was Dona Maria's recipe.

I was sitting at the kitchen island, watching the way his body moved as he cleaned up after insisting he do so since I'd made dinner. When my mobile vibrated with a call from Ares, I cringed. Given it was zero two hundred in the UK, it had to be something urgent.

"What's happened?" I asked after saying hello.

"We've received intel about a trafficking ring operating in the San Luis Obispo area. The anonymous tip we're currently trying to trace warned that the traffickers would have a presence at the upcoming fundraiser."

"The Wicked Winemakers' Ball?" The event was less than a week away, and Tryst and I had discussed going but hadn't made a final decision on whether or not we would.

"Affirmative. Can you mobilize a team?"

"Affirmative," I repeated back to him. "I'll make arrangements to travel to San Luis Obispo tomorrow."

Tryst studied me with scrunched eyes when I ended the call and repeated everything Ares said.

"I've scheduled the large-animal vet to be at the riding center today. Many of the animals require annual vaccinations. I will call and postpone in the morning."

"Don't do that, Tryst. I'll fly up in the morning and get started, then when you're finished, you can join me."

He walked over and pulled me to my feet. "I am not ready to be away from you. I've grown accustomed to us breathing the same air."

I smiled. "It will only be for a day or two."

"Only?"

I cupped each of his cheeks. "Perhaps we could make the time before I leave as fulfilling as we can."

"I am in agreement, but there is something I want to discuss with you before we get started." He winked.

He rarely preceded a conversation by saying we needed to have one. "What is it, Tryst?"

"I would like for us to be open about our love for each other, but I will not do so if it makes you uncomfortable."

"I would like that as well."

While our lovemaking was rushed before dinner, afterward we took our time, bringing each other as much pleasure as we could, late into the night.

When the time came for him to take me to the airport in Alamos, a feeling of foreboding washed over me. I did my best to tamp it down, but Tryst noticed.

"You are troubled. I will make arrangements for someone else to work with the vet today and travel with you."

"I'll be okay. I promise. And I'll feel better once I have the team assembled and we have crafted our plan for the event."

While I tried hard to reassure Tryst, by the time I boarded the plane, the feeling was significantly worse.

24

Tryst

I was about to arrange for my own flight to California when I received a call from my niece, Alex, saying she was on her way to the ranch.

"I'll be there in less than thirty minutes," she said when I asked when she planned to arrive. "I just got off the plane."

I shook my head and chuckled when I ended the call. Alex had been a force of nature since the day she was born. Like a hurricane.

I called Jaicon to let her know I might be delayed another day. "I promise to make it up to you, my love."

Like with everything, Jaicon did not complain but made my heart happy when she confessed how much she missed me. I could not fathom a life without her in it and expressed my thanks for her every time I prayed.

I was overjoyed when Alex said she'd be returning to California later the same day, and sent Jacy a message with the update. As soon as I had, I called a friend and made arrangements for a very special place for her and me to stay at while we were on the Central Coast. I'd thought of it many times and knew she'd love it.

I had spent so little time with Jada since Jaicon arrived in Mexico, but seeing her now, filled my heart with joy. She'd returned to the ranch in February, aimless and, like me at the time, without a sense of purpose. Since, she'd made great progress in her mental and emotional recovery, and now blossomed.

She'd graduated from law school in the States but hadn't taken the bar, unsure if she wanted to. In the eight months she'd been here, she'd completed the work she needed to do in order to be able to practice law in Mexico. Her chosen specialty was to become an immigration attorney so she could help those like the human trafficking victims to not fall vulnerable to people who would exploit them.

I knew she and Zin loved each other very much, and it broke my heart that they hadn't found their way back into one another's arms. I prayed that, like Jaicon and me, they would one day soon.

I'd always considered the flight from Alamos to San Luis Obispo to be quick. Today, the time dragged. I was like a child on Christmas morning when we landed, so anxious to get to Butler Ranch, where I knew Jaicon waited, and hold her in my arms.

Instead, when we deboarded, my love was waiting for me at the terminal gate. I raced over to her, gathered her in my arms, and kissed her.

"Um, kids, your PDA is drawing a crowd in the airport," said Alex, teasing us.

"Go away, Alexis," I said before kissing Jacy again.

"Did you know about this?" I heard her ask Jada, but I tuned out whatever her answer was. By tomorrow night, everyone would know, and I couldn't wait to share and celebrate our love.

"I have a car if you need a lift," Jaicon offered.

"I left mine here, so Jada and I will leave you two love birds on your own," said Alex. "Although you might want to get a room," she added under her breath.

Jaicon drove up the coast, and when we reached the turnoff for Butler Ranch, I told her to keep going and that I'd give her directions as we went. She glanced over at me and smiled but didn't ask where I was taking her. I loved that about her. Her sense of adventure, the way she trusted me, her faith in me.

"I missed you so," I said, reaching over to put my hand on her leg.

"Next time, I won't argue when you want to postpone an appointment. I missed you too."

We continued another twenty miles north on Pacific Coast Highway. "There will be a sign in another half mile. You will know to turn there." She raised a brow, but again, she didn't ask.

She smiled when she saw the sign I referenced. *"El Lugar de Curación North,"* she said, reading the hand-drawn sign affixed to the mile marker near the turnoff. We took the dirt road a few more yards and stopped in front of our cottage-by-the-sea getaway.

We exited the vehicle and came together, embracing as we took in the sweeping ocean views.

"This place belongs to Charlie Jenson," I explained.

"He is one of the *viejos*, yes?"

I nodded, kissing her temple. "I love you," I murmured.

She turned to face me. "And I love you." She cupped my cheek with her hand. "And while the view of the shoreline is spectacular, there is another I've been craving."

"I believe we may have the same craving."

The next night, I sat at the table at the Wicked Winemakers' Ball, reliving our lovemaking of yesterday and last night. When my eyes met Jacy's, I could tell she was thinking of the same thing.

As I'd anticipated, my family and our friends were overjoyed to learn she and I were together. While that announcement didn't seem to surprise anyone, they were all stunned to hear we were living together in a house I'd built on another part of my ranch. The only person not surprised was Brix, who'd helped me construct it.

I took a sip from the glass of Cabernet Sauvignon that the waiter set in front of me, shuddering as I recalled making love to Jaicon with my mouth the night before. "This is the wine I crave," I'd said, making her come with my tongue.

As much as I wanted us to relax and enjoy the evening, Jaicon was working. She and her team were positioned around the ballroom, communicating through a comms system. The majority of Los Caballeros wore the headsets too. It would more likely be one of us who noticed someone who seemed out of place at the event or someone none of us recognized. The Central Coast of California wine region was large in terms of square miles, but operated like any small town where the residents lived and worked together.

I turned to the stage when Alex announced the start of the bachelor auction. As during previous years, the bids for dates with the single billionaire winemakers escalated quickly, raising thousands of dollars for the local children's hospital.

"Ladies, I'm thrilled to open the bidding for a date with a man who is a fan favorite year after year: Zin Oliver!" I heard Alex say several bachelors later.

While she'd made the announcements, she didn't appear to be paying attention when people around the room began raising their paddles.

"Where is she?" I heard her ask her assistant, then she quickly turned off her mic. My eyes met Jaicon's. In them, I saw the same worry that something was wrong.

Seconds later, Zin jumped from the stage and ran, weaving his way through the crowd of people.

"The office!" he said through the comms.

"Suspect reported in back office. Possible hostage situation," I heard someone else say.

"Who is the hostage?" Jaicon asked, already running in that direction.

"Jada Yáñez," the voice responded.

Fear for Jada put me in a state of shock. I jumped up and raced in the same direction I saw several other people, all either part of Jaicon's team or my fellow *caballeros*, were going.

"Support needed in rear hallway of the building," Jaicon's voice came through the comms.

I entered the hallway at the same time I heard her voice yell, "*Freeze!* Hands in the air!"

Seconds later, Zin raced from the room with Jada in his arms at the exact moment I heard a gunshot. I rushed into the room, saying a prayer of thanks that it wasn't Jaicon who had been hit. Instead, I saw her and Tank kneeling on the floor by someone I recognized. His name was Harry Crosby, a man I'd known and despised for decades.

Jaicon was on the phone, calling for an ambulance, when Tank raised his head.

"There's no gun. No weapon of any kind," he said.

"Sorry, what did you say?" she asked.

"He was unarmed, Jaicon."

25

Jaicon

"Come with me," said Tryst, taking my hand.

"I cannot. I need to wait for emergency services."

"I got it," said Tank. "Go ahead."

Tryst led me out the back exit of the building and over to a lawn where picnic tables were set up.

"Look at me, Jaicon. Focus your eyes on mine."

Only then did I realize I hadn't looked at him. Not once since I shot an unarmed man. My eyes filled with the kind of tears that would make me feel weak if they were witnessed by anyone other than Tryst.

"He was unarmed," I whispered. "I shot a man who did not have a firearm. No weapon of any kind. Thank God he's still alive. If he'd died…" I couldn't allow myself to think about it. It would mean the end of my career. All my years of hard work would have been for naught. I shook my head and looked down at the ground. "He was unarmed. How could I have gotten things so wrong?" I said under my breath.

Tryst took both my hands in his. "Close your eyes."

I did as he asked.

"Tell me everything you saw. Start at the beginning."

I began when Tank met me at the office door and I asked him to break it in.

"I drew my gun and told Zin to cover Jada. Then I gave a count of three. Once inside, I shouted for the man in the room to freeze and to put his hands in the air."

"What happened next?" he asked.

"The bastard stepped behind Jada."

"And then?"

"Zin grabbed Jada and removed her from the room. That was when he reached for his weapon, and I fired."

"Keep your eyes closed and show me his movements."

I did from the moment we entered the office until my shot hit and he dropped.

"Open your eyes and tell me this. If Tank had done everything you did, exactly the way you did it, would you consider it a justifiable use of force?"

"I would," I responded without needing to think about it. "If he told the man to freeze, told him to put his hands in the air, and he did neither, then proceeded to reach anywhere, Tank would've had no choice but to fire."

Tryst gathered me in his arms, and I rested my head on his chest. "Once you have recovered from the shock of the last hour's events, I will tell you what I know about Harry Crosby."

I studied him. "What do you mean?"

"We will talk after you have had the chance to recover, Jacy. You are in shock."

When he held my hand, I realized it was shaking. "Okay."

"Now, you'll need to give a statement to Vader," said Tryst, motioning to the man walking in our direction. He was dressed in a tuxedo like Tryst was. The name sounded familiar to me, but I couldn't place it.

"Who is he?"

"The San Luis Obispo county sheriff."

"Hello," I said when he approached.

He held out his hand. "I'm Sheriff Conrad Krouse, but everyone calls me Vader. Do you feel up to giving me a statement?"

"I do."

He sat down and took out a notepad and pen. "Whenever you're ready."

As I had with Tryst, I closed my eyes. I went back further than I had earlier, beginning with Alex's announcement that Zin would be the next bachelor on the stage.

"Got it," he said when I stopped talking and opened my eyes.

"You are aware the K19 team received intelligence suggesting known traffickers would be in attendance this evening?" said Tryst.

Vader nodded. "And you know we've been trying to nail Crosby for years."

"What for?" I asked, looking between the two men.

"Back then, the term human trafficking wasn't as widely used as forced labor and sexual exploitation, but it all means the same thing." Vader looked at Tryst. "Me and the boys have been tryin' to catch the fucker for years."

"Your instincts were sound, my love," Tryst said after Vader walked away.

Two weeks later, when Harry Crosby died from sepsis brought on by an infection in the area where my bullet hit him, I wasn't so sure my instincts had been.

26

Tryst

Jaicon and I returned to *El Lugar de Curación* two days after the Wicked Winemakers' fundraiser. When we got the news of Crosby's death, she received a request from the sheriff to return to California. Since the investigation had transitioned from a shooting to murder, Jaicon would be deposed by the county's district attorney. No one believed she'd be charged. However, she still faced the inquisition.

Now, for the second time in a year, an emergency meeting was called, requesting the Los Caballeros *viejos* gather at the wine cave.

Brix and I stood at the head of the table, waiting for the current and past members to take their seats.

"I have gathered all of you together this evening to request the help of both the young *caballeros* and the old." I looked around the room, meeting the eyes of each person seated, then those standing. They nodded in response.

"As you are aware, Harry Crosby was shot at the Wicked Winemakers' Ball held on the twenty-first of October. Yesterday, he passed away."

Brix read the coroner's statement for the cause of death.

"Crosby has been on our radar for years," said Malcolm Warwick, shaking his head in disgust. "We've never been able to pin anything on him."

"That is the reason I've asked all of you to be here tonight. This has become personal to me. Together, I believe we will find the proof we need to prove what we've all known for decades. Los Caballeros, we must."

"What about Varilla?" asked Press. "You and Jaicon visited him in prison, yes?"

"He was uncommunicative."

"Perhaps he'd feel differently now Crosby is dead."

I studied Press. Maybe he was on to something. At the very least, he might have a reaction we could catch before he masked it.

"Why don't you let Kick and me talk to him?" said my nephew Salazar, who everyone called Snapper, pointing to his brother Rascon. "You and Jaicon could observe."

It was a good idea, and I said so. "I will talk with her about it and see what can be arranged."

"I've been thinking about this," said Charlie Jenson, who'd allowed Jacy and me to stay in his seaside cottage both for the ball and now. "What do we know about Crosby? He had open access to high-school-age kids for almost thirty years. That included the families of vineyard workers."

Martin Barrett raised his head. "I overheard someone talking about him after he was shot. They said something about how the man tutored children of migrant families."

"Who was it?" Brix asked.

"Robert Mancini."

I recognized the name. He'd purchased a vineyard property and winery located on the south side of Paso Robles only three or four years ago.

"I'll see what I can find out from him," Brix offered.

"I'll go with you," said Ridge.

"There may be a connection between him and Varilla," Charlie suggested.

Before we could enter into a discussion about his suggestion, my phone rang. "Excuse me. It's Vader," I said. The room went quiet.

"Hey, Tryst, my department received an anonymous tip about a murder. The caller gave us an address I thought sounded familiar. Turns out it's where Varilla was living when Luisa Reeve was abducted. The deputies on the scene confirmed two victims, both deceased. I'm headed there now, if you and Jaicon want to meet me there."

"We will do so. Thank you, Vader."

While I didn't have the phone on speaker, those closest to me had overheard the reason for the sheriff's call.

Brix put his hand on my shoulder. "Looks like we have a lead, Uncle."

"Many thanks to all of you here tonight. I will be in contact as soon as we know more."

27

Jaicon

"Are you hungry, lass?" Sorcha asked as I waited at Butler Ranch for Tryst's meeting with Los Caballeros to end.

"I am not, but thank you," I said, smiling at the woman who made it her mission to feed anyone who visited.

"I never liked Harry Crosby," she said, almost as though she was talking to herself. "There was always something about that man…"

"How did you know him?"

"He taught at the local high school, but not to my bairns."

Thus far, everyone I'd talked to about the man said they found him suspicious. What we needed was evidence they were right.

"Tryst has just arrived at the gate," Laird said, coming in from the front porch.

I was surprised his meeting had concluded so quickly. However, I was stunned when he raced inside.

"Vader called a few minutes ago. Two bodies were found at the house on Calle Caliente."

"Where Varilla lived for a while, yes?"

"Correct. He's headed there now and asked if we could meet him."

Vader met us at the front door. "The exterior of the home is meant to look like this might be a condemned property. The inside tells a different story."

He led us to a living room, where there was a sofa, chairs, and a large flat-screen television, along with end and coffee tables.

"Follow me," he said.

We walked down a hallway. Doors were open on either side, where deputies were searching the standard-looking bedrooms.

When we reached the end, the sheriff pulled up a piece of carpeting, revealing a trap door. "This leads to what started out as a crawl space."

We climbed down a ladder attached to the wall. Once at the bottom, I saw the space had been dug out to create something more like a basement. Metal brackets were attached to the cinder block walls. Crime scene tape surrounded two of them, where blood stains covered the dirt floor beneath two bodies.

"Cause of death was exsanguination—massive blood loss—and suffocation after their trachea were severed when their throats were slit," the coroner said to Vader when we walked over to him as he examined one of the victims.

"Their teeth were extracted with pliers"—he held up a pair—"and their fingerprints were burned off."

Vader motioned to other areas in the space. "My guys collected quite a bit of potential DNA evidence. One of them took it to the lab, who's working on it now."

"We know these men," Tryst said.

He was right. They were two of the five Felixstowe victims who'd left Tryst's ranch, saying they were headed to the US border. Two more of the group had been found murdered in La Higuera. That meant of the five, one remained.

"What about throughout the rest of the house? Any other evidence of who's been here?"

"Sir, I found something," said the deputy we'd seen in one of the bedrooms. "Ma'am, sir," he said, nodding to Tryst and me.

We followed him up the ladder and into a room where a mattress had been flipped and cut open. Inside was a duffel bag containing several bundles of money.

"We did a quick estimate, and it looks like there might be as much as two hundred thousand here."

Tryst looked at me. "If I were a man on the run, I wouldn't have left this behind," he said.

"Agreed." Which meant there was a chance the fifth man would return.

Vader arranged for deputies to stake out the house. Tryst, some of the other caballeros, and I took shifts, joining them, along with Tank, Blackjack, and Atticus.

On the third night, we watched someone approach the house and open a side gate.

"Let's move out," I heard Vader say through the comms.

"I'm going with them," I told Tryst, strapping on one of the two Kevlar vests we'd brought with us. "I love you, Tryst," I said before donning my NVGs.

"I'm right behind you, and I love you, my Jaicon," he said. I wanted to argue and tell him to remain in the vehicle, but there wasn't time.

"On the count of three," said Vader once I was in position with the rest of the team.

Three deputies, Tank, Blackjack, Atticus, and I cleared the house, including the crawl space. I got to the door of the bedroom where the money had been found in the mattress just as the man we'd seen enter through the side gate climbed out the window.

"Freeze!" I yelled, but not quickly enough to get a shot off. "Suspect exited the front window of bedroom three," I said through the comms, racing out after him.

As soon as my feet hit the ground, terror spread throughout my body. Tryst stood near the front door with the man's gun pressed against his temple. Even through the NVGs, I saw his eyes dart back and forth as if he was trying to tell me no.

"I got this," said Tank through the comms. "Ten seconds."

I didn't care—couldn't care—if Tank's shot killed him. All that mattered was for Tryst to live. "Do not fire unless you are certain you can take him out before he pulls the trigger. My life depends on it," I whispered.

"Give me my fucking money, or I kill him," the man shouted.

I counted the seconds as if they were hours. Praying to God and the deities that Tank would save the man I loved.

I could see him move into position in the bushes of the house next door. "Three, two, one," he said in quick succession.

I let out the breath I was holding when the man dropped to the ground, the gun in his hand falling with him.

I pulled the NVGs from my head and threw them down as I raced into Tryst's arms. At the same time, Blackjack and Atticus rushed to the man, securing his weapon.

I put my hands on either side of Tryst's face and kissed him, stopping only long enough to say, "Thank God you're okay."

"I am fine, my love," he said, tightening his arms around me.

"Call a bus," Atticus shouted. "The fucker's alive."

Epilogue

Tryst

Two weeks later

The man who'd held the gun to my head started talking while still recovering in the hospital from a non-life-threatening gunshot wound, mainly because he was far more afraid of Varilla's henchmen than he was of law enforcement. Since he had a price on his head, he didn't even try to negotiate a deal. All he wanted was to live.

From him, we learned that his boss, Harry Crosby, had been the ringleader of an extensive trafficking organization that had operated out of the Central Coast of California for decades. When Manual Varilla arrived, a turf war ensued between him and Crosby.

He also confirmed that some of the containers liberated in Felixstowe belonged to his boss and some to the other organization. The only thing he didn't seem to know was who Varilla worked for.

Having that much to go on, though, gave the UN coalition teams something to sink their teeth into, as they say.

"Press, Luisa, Zin, and Jada, along with their friends and family, will arrive later today," I said, walking up behind Jaicon and wrapping my arms around her waist as she prepared our breakfast.

Tomorrow, I would officiate the double ceremony of two best friends marrying two best friends. My heart was full of joy, but not just because of the wedding.

Jaicon carried two plates to the table from where we could look out at the El Pomar valley.

She returned to the kitchen and filled two glasses of freshly squeezed orange juice. "No coffee for me today," she said over her shoulder when I poured myself a cup.

"No?"

"Juice is fine."

I sat down next to her and breathed in the scent of the vegetable omelets she'd made for us. "This looks wonderful, my love. Thank you." I leaned over and kissed her.

"So, I have something to tell you."

"And I, you. Would you mind if I went first?"

Her eyes scrunched, but she nodded.

I stood and pushed my chair out of the way, then moved hers so she was facing me.

"You don't want to finish breakfast first?" she asked, giggling when I parted her legs and knelt between them.

Her expression sobered when I took both of her hands in mine. "You have brought me back to life, my beloved Jaicon. My love for you is the reason I wake up each morning with a sense of peace and a full heart. 'I love you' doesn't seem adequate to describe the depth of what I feel for you."

Jaicon's eyes flooded, but a smile spread across her face when I pulled a small box from my pocket.

"Will you make me the happiest man alive and marry me?" I asked, opening the box to show her the ring I'd had made for her.

She put her hands on either side of my face as tears streamed down her cheeks. "Yes, yes, yes, I will marry you."

I slipped the ring on her finger and kissed her. "What did you want to tell me, my love?"

She gripped both my hands in hers and stared into my eyes. "We're going to have a baby, Tryst."

"We are?" I said, my voice choked with emotion.

She nodded as more tears ran down her cheeks.

We hadn't been trying to conceive, but we hadn't been using birth control either. Both of us agreed if we were blessed with a baby, we'd be thrilled, and if we weren't, our love would be enough.

"A baby," I repeated, closing my eyes and saying a prayer of thanks.

"A baby," she repeated. "Our baby."

Keep reading for a sneak peek at the
next book in Heather Slade's
K19 Allied Intelligence Team One series,

Code Name: Poseidon

**He's the only man who sees past her deadly facade.
She's the woman who holds his heart captive.
Together, they'll discover that love
is worth more than revenge.**

POSEIDON

As a seasoned intelligence agent, I thought I'd seen it all. But when Oleander, the woman who broke my heart years ago, reenters my life, I'm thrust into a dangerous world of human trafficking and personal vendettas. As we work together to take down the shadowy organization known as AMPS, I find myself falling for her all over again. But can I trust her with my heart when she's hiding so many secrets? With every mission, the stakes get higher, and I'm forced to confront a terrifying question: Will our love survive the dangerous game we're playing, or will Oleander's quest for revenge consume us both?

OLEANDER

For years, I've lived and breathed one mission: to destroy AMPS, the trafficking ring responsible for my parents' deaths. I never expected to cross paths with Poseidon again, the man I left behind at Sandhurst. Now, as we join forces in a UN coalition, I'm torn between my thirst for vengeance and the undeniable pull of our rekindled connection. With each revelation about my past and every confrontation with our enemies, I'm forced to question everything I believed. Can I trust Poseidon with the truth of who I really am? And when the dust settles, will there be anything left of me beyond the revenge that's defined my life for so long?

1

Poseidon

"I *know* it's her," said Oleander. "I don't know why I didn't consider Pharaoh could be a woman."

While the name had been linked with Mithras, we had no proof the two worked together or hard evidence there was a person who went by the name.

When Oleander and Verity found an offshore account belonging to a shell corp called AMPS Inc. at a bank in Mauritius linked to an account they believed belonged to Mithras, they began theorizing about the acronym.

Doing so was part of our job. Going with our gut, following a hunch, and tracking leads were part of our training to be an intelligence officer. An equal part of what we did for a living was our "intuition" leading us to a dead end.

"On the other hand, she could be either "A" or "S," I said.

Oleander shifted in my arms, her hardened nipples brushing my skin, and I was instantly rock hard. It hadn't been fifteen minutes since I was brought to my most recent mind-blowing orgasm at the hands and mouth of the woman who excited me to the point of distraction whenever she was close enough for me to breathe in her uniquely erotic scent.

The combination of jasmine, saffron, cedarwood, and ambergris was as addicting as the woman herself. Something I should well remember led to harmful consequences. My attraction to Oleander was as pervasive and intense as a dependence to a drug I knew would lead to my ruin, yet I couldn't resist her.

I rose, flipped to her to stomach, and grabbed her hips, positioning her so I had complete access to her pussy and ignored the clench in my gut, reminding me my need for this woman would be my categorical ruin.

About the Author

USA Today best-selling author Heather Slade writes shamelessly sexy, edge-of-your seat romantic suspense.

She gave herself the gift of writing a book for her own birthday one year. Sixty-plus books later (and counting), she's having the time of her life.

The women Slade writes are self-confident, strong, with wills of their own, and hearts as big as the Colorado sky. The men are sublimely sexy, seductive alphas who rise to the challenge of capturing the sweet soul of a woman whose heart they'll hold in the palm of their hand forever. Add in a couple of neck-snapping twists and turns, a page-turning mystery, and a swoon-worthy HEA, and you'll be holding one of her books in your hands.

She loves to hear from her readers. You can contact her at heather@heatherslade.com

To keep up with her latest news and releases, please visit her website at www.heatherslade.com to sign up for her newsletter.

MORE FROM AUTHOR HEATHER SLADE

**WINE COUNTRY
ROMANCE**

**COWBOY
ROMANCE**

BUTLER RANCH
Kade's Worth
Brodie's Promise
Maddox's Truce
Naughton's Secret
Mercer's Vow
Kade's Return
Butler Ranch Christmas

**WICKED WINEMAKERS
CENTRAL COAST
FIRST LABEL**
Brix's Bid
Ridge's Release
Press' Passion
Zin's Sins
Tryst's Temptation

**WICKED WINEMAKERS
CENTRAL COAST
SECOND LABEL**
Beau's Beloved
Cru's Crush
Bit's Bliss
Snapper's Seduction
Kick's Kiss

**WICKED WINEMAKERS
RUSSIAN RIVER VALLEY
FIRST LABEL**
Bas' Blend
Hux's Harvest
Wolf's Want
Oak's Vintage
Cooper's Claim

**COWBOYS OF
CRESTED BUTTE**
A Cowboy Falls
A Cowboy's Dance
A Cowboy's Kiss
A Cowboy Stays
A Cowboy Wins

ROARING FORK RANCH
Roaring Fork Wrangler
Roaring Fork Roughstock
Roaring Fork Rockstar
Roaring Fork Rooker
Roaring Fork Bridger

SANGRE VISTA RANCH
Thorn's Stand
Stetson's Storm
Maverick's Reckoning
Cinch's Wager
Flints Chance

www.ingramcontent.com/pod-product-compliance
Lightning Source LLC
Chambersburg PA
CBHW070624300726
48975CB00006B/1912